T0365910

Forever Friends

Ann Westmoreland

authorHOUSE®

AuthorHouse™
1663 Liberty Drive
Bloomington, IN 47403
www.authorhouse.com
Phone: 1 (800) 839-8640

Published by AuthorHouse   03/12/2015

ISBN: 978-1-5049-0031-7 (sc)
ISBN: 978-1-5049-0050-8 (e)

Print information available on the last page.

Any people depicted in stock imagery provided by Thinkstock are
models, and such images are being used for illustrative purposes only.
Certain stock imagery © Thinkstock.

This book is printed on acid-free paper.

Because of the dynamic nature of the Internet, any web addresses or
links contained in this book may have changed since publication and
may no longer be valid. The views expressed in this work are solely those
of the author and do not necessarily reflect the views of the publisher,
and the publisher hereby disclaims any responsibility for them.

Chapter One

The Attic

"King me!" Jenny called out as she moved her black checker to the end of the checkerboard.

Calvin frowned as he put the last black checker he had won from Jenny on hers. "Let's do something else." This was the third game in a row that he lost to Jenny, and he was anxious to change what they were doing.

"You just want to quit 'cause I'm winning," Jenny accused.

"No, I'm just tired of checkers. Three games are enough for me."

Outside, lightning streaked across the afternoon sky, and thunder rattled the windows. Jenny shivered from the noise and then said excitedly, "I know what we can do!" She jumped up, ran to the stairs, and darted up two steps at a time, with Calvin on her heels. Once upstairs, she turned left and headed for her Uncle Paul's room. Turning the knob, not bothering to knock, she entered and told Calvin, "Uncle Paul's at work at the hotel. He usually works nights, but he had to go in early today."

"Why are we going in his room? What's in there?" Calvin asked as he ran up beside her.

"The attic door is in here."

"The attic door is in his room?" Calvin scrunched his eyebrows.

"It's really in his closet," Jenny explained.

"His closet?"

"Yeah. Cool, huh? It's just like in 'The Lion, The Witch, and The Wardrobe."

"What's in the attic?" Calvin asked.

"All sorts of cool stuff."

Jenny opened Uncle Paul's closet door and switched on the light switch on the wall behind his brown jacket. She opened the door to the attic. A musty smell drifted up their nostrils.

"What kind of stuff?" Calvin asked, as lightning flashed through the bedroom window.

"Everything that no one knows what to do with," she told Calvin. "Come on, you'll see." She raced up the attic stairs.

At the top of the stairs, Calvin and Jenny looked around at a vast array of old trunks, toys, pictures, and an assortment of forgotten treasures. Over to the right, under the window, sat several old pictures and portraits of her grandparents, her Great Aunt Annie, and one of her father and Uncle Paul when they were boys. On the other side stood an old bedroom set that her grandfather had made, Marylou and Jenny's old highchair, crib, and jumping horse, worn from many happy hours of use.

"Let's start with Uncle Paul's old trunk," Jenny suggested. "The uniform that he wore to military school is in there." She opened an old black trunk with gold strapping and gold handles.

"Wow!" Calvin exclaimed. "This is cool! It looks like he was in the army, or something." He pulled out a brown jacket and tried it on. "He must have been about my age when he wore this. Look. It's just my size." Calvin turned around for Jenny to see. He picked up a hat, which looked like what a general would wear, and put it on. It slid down over his eyes. Jenny laughed. Calvin took it off and said, "The hat's a little big, though."

Lightning flashed through the window, followed immediately by a loud clap of thunder. Jenny spun around. "What's that!" she cried out, as she looked over at the corner by the window.

"What's what? The thunder?"

"No, the other noise."

"What other noise?" Calvin asked.

"The one over there," Jenny whispered, as she pointed toward the old pictures.

"Let's look," Calvin suggested. "Maybe it's a ghost."

"We don't have ghosts up here," Jenny said.

"How do you know?" Calvin taunted. "Didn't you say that both your grandparents and your Great Aunt Annie died in this house? Maybe some of their ghosts live up here?"

"No, they don't. Aunt Annie's in Heaven, remember?" Jenny referred to the time last year when her aunt had been given permission to come back to give her piano lessons in the middle of the night. At first, only Jenny was allowed to see her, but Calvin was allowed to visit on her last night back.

"How do you know your grandparents' ghosts aren't here?" Calvin asked.

"I just know," Jenny answered nervously, as thunder rattled the wooden beams in the ceiling and shook the windowpanes of the attic window.

"Maybe you just haven't seen them," Calvin said, with a glint of mischief in his voice. He liked to stir things up whenever he could. "They probably have always been up here. Maybe…"

"Oh, hush," Jenny whispered. "You don't know that. Listen. There it is again. I know you heard that."

"Yeah. I think it came from behind that picture of the old lady. Let's look," Calvin suggested. He walked

5

over to the pictures and pulled out a dusty portrait of a gray haired old lady, wearing a long, black dress.

Jenny peered behind the pictures. "There's nothing here," she said, disappointment sounding in her voice. She loved action, too. Jenny and Calvin had been friends since she moved into this house after her great aunt died. The friends had found they had the same interests, most of them action-packed. Wherever one found Jenny, Calvin was usually there, too.

"Yes, there is," Calvin teased. "You just can't see all ghosts."

"The noise doesn't sound like a ghost." Jenny tried to reassure Calvin as well as herself. She hadn't been afraid of ghosts since Aunt Annie had come back from Heaven, but then again, she had only met one ghost. There could be more that weren't as loving as Aunt Annie.

"You don't know that," Calvin said. "If you did, you wouldn't be so nervous."

"I'm not nervous."

"Yes, you are." Calvin was still trying to stir things up.

"Besides," Jenny went on, "if there were ghosts up here, wouldn't we have heard them before now, especially at night?" With that, she spun around and walked quickly back to the trunk. Let's put the uniform back and go downstairs. Argo baked some chocolate chip cookies this morning.

Argo was Jenny's nanny. She came to take care of Jenny and her sister, Marylou, after their mother died when Jenny was two. Jenny and Marylou loved Argo, almost as much as they would have loved their mother. Argo felt the same way about the girls.

Before Calvin could reply, a brown streak scampered across his shoe. "What's that?" he shouted.

"What's what?" Jenny asked. She turned to face Calvin.

"That," Calvin said, as he pointed to a brown ball of fur under the highchair.

"It's a squirrel," Jenny whispered. "Isn't it cute?" She peered under the highchair.

"A squirrel?" Calvin shouted.

"Shh." Jenny put her finger to her lips. "Not so loud."

"Why?"

"Argo will be up here with a broom."

"So."

"So, she'll try to kill it," Jenny replied.

"Why would she want to kill it?" Calvin scrunched his eyebrows together.

"She doesn't like mice in the house. She kills them."

"Why would she kill a squirrel? It's not a mouse."

"It's a rodent," Jenny explained. "Mice are rodents, too. She hates mice, so she'd probably hate squirrels, too."

"Oh." Calvin didn't really understand Jenny's reasoning. Squirrels were a lot different from mice.

"Let's open the window," Jenny suggested. "It'll probably go out when it stops raining."

"I don't think so," Calvin replied softly. He looked down into a box sitting by an old nightstand, before he bent over and picked it up.

"Why?" Jenny asked.

"Look in here." Calvin poked the box toward Jenny. Nestled in the box, with Aunt Annie's old hats, were four baby squirrels, with their eyes still closed.

"Oh, they're so-oo cute!" Jenny squealed. "Let's bring them downstairs and show them to my dad."

Jenny's dad was sitting by the fireplace reading a book. He glanced up when Jenny and Calvin ran into the room, the military school uniform flying out behind Calvin. "What's up kids? Playing dress-up?" he asked.

"No. Look," she said as she thrust the box onto his lap. "We found them in the attic."

"Don't touch them," he cautioned.

"Why? Will they bite?" Jenny asked.

"Probably not. But if you do touch them, their mother might not have anything to do with them again," Mr. Jenkins explained. "She may abandon them."

"Why?" Jenny and Calvin asked together.

"It's just what many wild animals do when they smell human scent on their young. I do know that birds abandon their young if a human touches their babies in a nest."

"I know what we can do!" Jenny said excitedly.

"What?" Mr. Jenkins asked.

"When it stops raining," Jenny said, "I'll crawl out my bedroom window onto the porch roof and put the box up near the point, right under the attic window. Someone can open the window in the attic so the mother squirrel can get out. When she hears her babies, she'll go to them. Then, we can shut the window, so she can't get back inside."

"But where will she take her babies if the window is shut?" Calvin asked. "She can't raise her babies in a hat box on the porch roof."

"I might be able to help with that," Mr. Jenkins said smiling. "Remember the bird house in the old apple tree in the back yard?"

"Yes. Why?" Jenny asked.

"I think," Mr. Jenkins said, "that it would make a fine house for a squirrel family."

"But the hole's too small," Jenny protested. "The babies would fit, but the mother squirrel wouldn't."

"If I cut the hole a little larger with my needle-nose saw, she would," Mr. Jenkins answered. "When it stops raining, I'll take it down from the apple tree, make the hole bigger, and hang it from the top branches of the chokecherry tree growing beside the porch. When the mother squirrel crawls out of the attic to investigate her babies, she'll be able to see it."

As though on cue, the rainstorm slowed up and stopped in the next few minutes. Their plan was put into action. Mr. Jenkins cut the hole in the birdhouse and hung it in the chokecherry tree. Then, he tiptoed up the attic stairs, slowly opened the attic window, and went back to the stairway to hide.

Meanwhile, Jenny crawled out of her bedroom window and onto the porch roof. She turned to Calvin, who was inside, and said, "Okay, hand me the box."

"Here you go," he said, gently handing it to her.

After pushing the box almost to the peak of the roof so it was right under the attic window, Jenny quickly slid back through her window and stood beside Calvin behind the curtains. All anyone could see of the children were their eyes peeking around the pink curtains. As they watched, they heard the babies making soft, squeaking noises, almost like mice.

"Look," Jenny whispered. She looked out the window and pointed up at the brick chimney.

Climbing cautiously down the outside of the chimney, the mother squirrel looked back and forth and up and down, trying to spot danger. Not seeing any, she scampered over to the box and peered in.

With Jenny and Calvin watching, awestruck, she climbed in and checked the babies all over with her nose. She pushed them this way and that, even rolling them over on their backs. Satisfied that they were not harmed in any way, she picked one up in her mouth and ran back up the side of the chimney, toward the attic window. Finding it closed tight, with Mr. Jenkins standing inside, she ran back down to the roof. She scampered back and forth, looking wide-eyed and confused. After several minutes of random scampering, she spotted the birdhouse.

"She sees it," Jenny whispered.

The mother squirrel put down her baby and stared at the house. Quick as a flash, she jumped into the tree, ran down a branch to the house, and checked it out, peering in and sitting on the little roof. She looked so comical that both Jenny and Calvin giggled softly.

"Look," Calvin whispered. "The baby's rolling."

"Oh, no," Jenny said quietly. Her voiced quivered. "It's going to fall."

"No, it's not," Calvin reassured her, "It'll probably go into the rain gutter."

"But it's full of water," Jenny cried softly.

Quickly, as if the mother squirrel sensed the danger her baby was in, she looked over on the roof, made a wild leap to land beside the tiny squirrel, and grabbed her baby at the back of its neck, just as it was rolling into the rain gutter.

"Whew," Jenny sighed, as she let out the breath she had been holding inside her.

The mother squirrel, with her baby in her mouth, jumped over into the chokecherry tree, ran down the branch, and deposited the tiny animal in the little house. She then ran out, jumped over to the roof, scrambled into the box, and picked up another baby, as she looked nervously from side to side. She then repeated her motions and deposited this baby, also. By the time she picked up her last baby, the mother squirrel seemed more confident. She tucked them into the house, then gathered leaves for bedding, dropped them into the hole, and scampered inside. She looked so content when she peered out the little hole and looked at Jenny and Calvin in the window, that Jenny and Calvin laughed.

"Supper's ready," Argo called up the stairs. "Calvin, your mom called and said it was time for you to go home. She said that your supper's ready, too."

Jenny and Calvin, suddenly hungry, ran down the stairs and jumped the last three to the floor. Argo heard them and commented, "Mercy, children, you're going to get hurt if you run down the stairs like that."

Jenny laughed. "We're fine, Argo. We always run down the stairs and jump the last three. It's fun!"

"I know, and I wish you wouldn't," Argo answered quietly.

Jenny knew that she only fussed at them because she cared.

"Let's go in the attic again sometime. That was fun," Calvin told Jenny at the front door.

"Okay, but not tomorrow. Marylou is having a birthday-slumber party, and I want to think up things to annoy her and her stuck-up friends."

"Cool. If you need any help, let me know," Calvin said. He loved to annoy Marylou. He leaped down the porch steps and ran across the yard to his house next door.

"I will," Jenny called back, smiling, knowing that she could always count on Calvin. He was the best friend she had ever had.

Chapter Two

The Slumber Party

"Ellen, have you met Tony?" Marylou asked, looking up from her sleeping bag. The living room was littered with sleeping bags of all colors, with fat pillows at one end of each. Cokes and popcorn were scattered around between the sleeping bags, and a pile of videos were in front of the television set.

"Tony who?" Ellen answered, holding her foot up. She painted her big toe with blue polish.

"That tall, unbelievably good-looking guy that moved in down the street," Marylou said.

"I've seen him in the hall at school, but I've never talked to him," Ellen answered.

"Is he the one with curly black hair and the big green eyes?" Lisa asked, tossing a handful of popcorn into her mouth.

"Yes!" Marylou answered. "Isn't he gorgeous? His voice is even sexy."

"You've talked to him? When?" Ellen asked, dropping her foot to the floor and stared wide-eyed at Marylou.

"At the bus stop." Marylou looked proud. "He only lives four doors down."

"Lucky!" Lisa cried enviously. "I wish someone like that would move into my neighborhood. All we get are losers."

"Losers? Like who?" Marylou asked.

"Like Charles 'Creep' Billings, who waddles when he walks. He wears his pants so low and his shirts so high, that his crack is always showing."

"Gross!" Suzie moaned. She stuck her lower lip out making a face.

"What's gross?" Jenny asked, bouncing into the room.

"Nothing you need to know about," Marylou answered. She turned her back to Jenny. "Besides, you wouldn't understand. Wait until you're older."

"Okay. Then I won't tell you that the pizza is ready."

"Pizza?" Lisa looked interested. "What kind?"

"Pepperoni and extra cheese, I think," Marylou answered.

"Good," Lisa said. "No anchovies or onions."

"Come and get it," Argo called from the kitchen.

Marylou and her friends jumped up running past Jenny to the kitchen. "Mmm. It smells so good. I didn't think I'd be hungry after all that ham I ate for supper," Marylou said.

While she watched the girls come back from the kitchen with plates of pizza, Jenny's mind whirled with things she could do to annoy them. She felt that they didn't even treat her human, that they were too good to even talk to her. Feeling they were stuck-up brats, she followed them back to the living room, peering around the corner to spy on them.

"Let's watch 'The Beast,'" Suzie said, as she picked up one of the videos Marylou and Mr. Jenkins had rented from The Red Box at Walmart.

"No. Let's see 'Love in the Afternoon' first," Cheri suggested.

"If we see 'The Beast' first, we won't be scared when we go to sleep," Suzie reasoned.

"Okay, okay," Marylou said. "I think I can settle this. Let's see the one about the man who dies, comes back to life as a dog, and lives with his own family; then we can see the others."

"Can I watch, too?" Jenny asked from the doorway.

"No!" chorused the girls.

"We don't want any little kids in here," Marylou said in an uppity voice.

Spinning around, tears stinging her eyes, Jenny ran out the front door and down the steps. Resolving to get them back for their hatefulness, she ran toward Calvin's house. She didn't stop until she rang his doorbell.

"Hi, Jenny. What's up?" Calvin asked. He pulled the inside door open and talked through the screen.

"Those stuck-up girls' noses, that's what." Jenny's eyes welled with tears, but she did not want to cry in front of Calvin.

"Do you still want to do something to them?" He was anxious to have some fun and irritate Marylou. She treated him like a little kid.

Calvin opened the screen door and walked out on the porch. He sat on the swing with his legs dangling. "We could put masks on and scare them."

"No," Jenny said as she sat down beside him. "They'd know it was us. They wouldn't be scared."

"We could cut off the main switch on the circuit breaker. I watched my dad do it at his house, when he put in a new electric line. Then, they'd be in the dark."

"No, Argo would just get mad. Her favorite show is on television tonight. She's going to watch it in her room, since Marylou and her stuck-up friends took over the living room."

"We could go into the attic and pretend we're ghosts, with chains and stuff. That would scare them."

"We can't do that, either. Uncle Paul is sleeping. He has to be at work at eleven o'clock tonight."

"I know!" Calvin shouted. "We could bring Slither over to your house. He'd scare them."

"Wow! That's a great idea. Marylou hates snakes, especially big ones like your ball python."

Calvin and Jenny jumped up and ran into the house. "Mom," Calvin called. "May I go over to Jenny's for awhile?"

"Sure, but be home by nine-thirty," Mrs. Kelly called from the kitchen. "You know school starts Tuesday, and you need to start getting to bed early."

Calvin and Jenny ducked into his bedroom and gathered up Slither. With the snake draped around Calvin's neck, they ran back to Jenny's house, slipping quietly through the front door.

"Shh," Jenny whispered, putting her finger across her lips. They tiptoed across the hall to the stairway and peered around the corner. The girls all sat on their sleeping bags facing the television set.

"Should I walk in like this?" Calvin asked.

"No, they wouldn't be scared," Jenny said. "They'd just yell at us and tell us to get out."

"What do you want to do then?"

"Let's put Slither down, and let him crawl into the room. That would really scare them, especially if they didn't see us," Jenny whispered.

"They might step on him." Calvin didn't want anything to happen to his snake.

"No, they wouldn't. They'll run away and scream."

"Okay," Calvin agreed. He took the reptile off his neck gently lowering it to the floor, stretching his arm around the corner of the wall before he let it go.

Slither, as though he was trained to do so, crawled soundlessly, straight to the sleeping bags. Lisa caught sight of him out of the corner of her eye and jerked her head around. She yelled at the top of her lungs, "A SNAKE!"

"A SNAKE!" chorused the other girls.

"Help!" Cheri yelled. She jumped on the sofa and sat on the back, hugging her arms tight around her chest.

"Help!" Marylou yelled. She jumped on the recliner and curled her feet under her.

"Help!" cried the other girls. They scrambled on whatever furniture was closest. Cokes, popcorn, and pizza spilled everywhere in their wake.

"Whatever is the matter?" Argo asked, as she rushed into the living room carrying a dish towel.

"There's a snake loose in here!" Marylou shrieked.

"A SNAKE!" Argo yelled, as she pulled her large body onto a very small piano stool and waved the towel in the air. "Help, someone! Anyone!" she screamed.

Mr. Jenkins, hearing the commotion, ran from his room where he had been watching a baseball game. "What's going on down there?" he called from the top of the stairs. Then, seeing Jenny and Calvin on the stairway, laughing helplessly and holding their sides, he became stern. He put his hands on his hips and asked, "All right, what did you two do now?"

"Us?" Jenny asked, trying to keep a straight face. Her cheeks bubbled with the laughter she was trying to keep inside.

"Yes, you," Mr. Jenkins said sternly. He knew his youngest daughter had done something. She kept everyone on their toes with her antics.

"What's all the noise down there?" Uncle Paul called sleepily, as he came out of his room. "Is the house on fire?"

"No, but Jenny and Calvin have done something to scare Argo and the girls," Mr. Jenkins answered.

"What have those two done now?" Uncle Paul asked, smiling. Sometimes he helped Jenny and Calvin pull some of their pranks. No one expected him to be in on them, so he could be the straight man in their antics.

"Jenny! Calvin! What have you two done?" Mr. Jenkins asked sternly.

"It's only my snake," Calvin said. "Those girls are afraid of a harmless, little pet snake."

"It's not little!" Argo yelled, still waving the towel like a flag. "It's a monster!"

"No he's not," Jenny said. "He's cute."

"Cute, my foot!" Argo yelled. "Come and get him, NOW!"

"Okay, but he won't hurt anybody," Jenny said. She walked into the living room, followed by Calvin, her father, and Uncle Paul.

"Where is he?" Calvin asked.

"I don't know," Marylou answered. "I was too busy getting away."

"He was by my sleeping bag," Lisa told them, from the back of Mr. Jenkins' favorite blue chair by the fireplace.

Jenny, Calvin, Uncle Paul, and Mr. Jenkins searched the room. They picked up sleeping bags, pillows, and small furniture. Jenny and Calvin looked under the sofa with a flashlight. All they saw was dust. Mr. Jenkins looked behind the bookcase, and Uncle Paul looked behind the television set. Everyone came up empty-handed.

"I'm not staying in this room another minute!" Marylou yelled. She stomped out of the living room, followed by her friends. "I'll get you for this," she hissed to Jenny, as she marched past her.

Still screaming, Argo yelled, "I'm leaving, too!" She carefully got down from the small piano stool; her eyes darted around the room, watching for any signs of the snake. Not seeing anything, she bolted out the front door to sit on the porch swing.

Marylou and her friends stomped off up the stairs, leaving all their sleeping bags, blankets, and pillows behind. "I'm not sleeping down there," Marylou said to no one in particular.

"There's snake slime on the sleeping bags," Cheri said.

"Coke soaked through mine," Suzie said.

"Ellen dropped her pizza upside-down on my sleeping bag, and Marylou stepped on my pillow," Lisa complained to Suzie.

Once upstairs, the girls stripped the linen closet of every blanket, pillow, and sheet. They covered Marylou's bedroom floor with them and turned the stereo up high, singing with the music.

Downstairs, Jenny asked, "Where can he be? It's not like he's too small to be seen. Could he have crawled outside?"

"Not unless he went up the chimney," Uncle Paul said. "You would have seen him crawl past you in the hallway."

"That's true," Calvin agreed, as he nodded his head.

"I'm not putting one foot into the house until you get that snake out of there!" Argo yelled from the front porch.

"Here he is," Uncle Paul said, picking up Marylou's sleeping bag. Snuggled way town at the bottom of the bag, Slither was curled into a ball, safe and warm.

"Whew, I'm glad you found him," Calvin said with relief. "I was getting worried." He unzipped the sleeping bag and pulled Slither out.

"It's almost nine-thirty," Jenny reminded him. "We don't want your mom mad at us, too."

"Thanks, I forgot about the time," Calvin said, bounding out the door, past Argo, and down the steps. Slither dangled around his neck.

Jenny and Argo watched Calvin run across their yard and into his, and then they went back into the house. Jenny ran upstairs and announced to Marylou and her friends, "We found the snake."

"Where was it?" Marylou asked.

"Uncle Paul found it at the bottom of your sleeping bag, all cuddled up," Jenny answered with a sly smile. She put her hands together and pretended to use them as a pillow against her cheek.

"Eeww, gross!" Marylou made a face. "I'm never, ever using it again. You can burn it, if you want. The snake germs will never come off."

"Snakes don't have germs," Jenny said.

"Yes, they do," Marylou said with authority.

"Can I have your sleeping bag, instead of burning it?" Jenny loved that bag. It was much softer than hers.

"Suit yourself," Marylou answered. "I don't care. I just know that I'll never sleep in it again. I'd always think of that snake."

"Marylou," Argo called up the stairs. "You and the girls can come down here again. The snake's gone."

"No," Marylou answered. "We're going to stay up here tonight. Our sleeping bags are full of pizza, Coke, and snake slime."

When Jenny went back downstairs, Argo was waiting for her with rags and carpet cleaner. "After you put a load of sleeping bags into the washer, you can clean the Coke off the carpet before it sets in," she said as she handed her the supplies.

"Oh, great," Jenny pouted.

"Oh, don't be so mad," Argo told her. "You have no one to blame but yourself."

""I know," Jenny said, taking the carpet cleaner, "but it was worth it." She loved to irritate Marylou.

"I'll help you," Uncle Paul offered. "I don't have to leave for work for almost an hour." He had enjoyed the trick as much as Jenny and Calvin.

"Thanks," Jenny said, handing him a load of sleeping bags. "If you put these in the washer, I'll clean the carpet."

Oh, well, Jenny thought. Maybe next year we can think of something even worse to do to Marylou on her birthday. Maybe I could put something like fresh dog mess in a burning paper bag. It would be so funny to watch her stomp it out.

Chapter Three

The Accident

"Do you realize that this is our last free Friday?" Jenny asked. Calvin and Jenny sat cross-legged in Calvin's tree house. There was a checker game between them. "Let's do something fun."

"Yeah. School starts Tuesday," Calvin answered. "I hope I don't get Miss Means. She scares me."

"Me, too," Jenny agreed. "I hope we both get Mrs. Sunnyfield. At least she smiles sometimes."

"Miss Means never smiles," Calvin said.

"Have you noticed that Miss Means looks just like a witch, with her long, skinny face and long, messy-looking hair?" Jenny asked. "Her fingers are just like the witches' in 'The Wizard of Oz'."

"Yeah," Calvin agreed. "Her long nose makes her even more witchy-looking."

"Brr," Jenny sad as shivers went up her back.

"Let's ride our bikes down to the creek and forget about her," Calvin suggested.

"Good idea. Wait here while I ask Argo."

"I have to tell my mom, too," Calvin said. "See if you can bring lunch with you. Mom went shopping yesterday, so I know we have chips and Cokes."

"Argo fixed ham for supper last night. I could probably make some sandwiches," Jenny said. "I think we still have some chocolate cake left over from Marylou's birthday party, if her stuck-up friends didn't eat it all."

"We sure scared them, didn't we?" Calvin said with a smile on his face. "That was fun."

"Yeah," Jenny agreed. "Well, let's get lunch. I'll meet you back here in ten minutes."

After asking Argo, Jenny quickly fixed two sandwiches. She was back in the yard before Calvin.

After he ran out the door and ran toward her, Jenny called out, "Those piggies did eat all of the cake, but I put extra ham in the sandwiches."

"Good. I brought barbeque potato chips and Cokes. Let's go," Calvin said. He hopped on his bike. He wrapped the top of a brown paper lunch bag around the handle and put his hand over it.

The creek ran along one side of Jenny's yard, but they followed it downstream until they came to a bend that was wider and deeper than the rest of the creek. The bridge on Malcolm Irving Road went right over the widest and deepest part. Usually people from the neighborhood fished from the bridge, but not today.

After getting off her bike, Jenny pulled off her sneakers and thrust her feet into the water. "Oo-oh. That feels so good," she said as she wiggled her toes. Two fish came over to investigate her feet.

Jenny and Calvin heard a sudden screech. "What's that?" Calvin yelled. He jumped up and looked toward the noise.

"It sounds like a car," Jenny said, looking toward the street.

"Look!" Calvin yelled. He pointed to the dark blue truck swerving in the road.

"It's Claudia!" screamed Jenny.

"Claudia?" Calvin asked. "Who's Claudia?"

"You know. She's the girl in the next block who has that big black dog."

"Oh. Yeah. I know who she is."

"Look at her truck! It's going off the road!" yelled Jenny. "She can't make the curve!"

"She's coming toward us!" Calvin screamed. He ran back up the bank of the creek.

Jenny yanked her feet out of the creek and scurried up the bank after Calvin, grabbing grass to help her move faster. "She's going in the creek!" she yelled, as the dark blue truck splashed into the water. They watched in horror as the truck hit the middle of the creek. It didn't sink right away. It just bobbed in the water.

"Is Claudia hurt?" Calvin asked.

"She's moving around. Look, she can't get the door open."

"Open the window!" Calvin shouted.

Claudia looked up when Calvin yelled. She opened the window. "Help me!" she called.

"What can we do?" Jenny asked.

"I don't know!" Claudia cried. "Is the water deep here?"

"It's the deepest part of the creek," Jenny answered.

"I'm sinking!" Claudia yelled, as water rushed in under the doors and lapped around her ankles.

"Come on!" Jenny yelled. "Get out of there!"

"Crawl out the window!" Calvin yelled.

Claudia climbed up and sat on the window opening. The truck was rapidly filling with water. She looked around for a second, and then she ducked back inside, grabbed her purse, and slid out feet first into the muddy, murky water. "I can't touch bottom!" she screamed.

"Can you swim?" Jenny asked.

"Yes," Claudia replied. She started moving toward Jenny and Calvin, still holding onto her purse.

"Here's a stick," Jenny said, as she picked up a long branch and thrust it quickly toward Claudia.

"Thanks," Claudia answered breathlessly, grabbing the branch.

Jenny and Calvin pulled on the branch, dragging Claudia out of the water. The truck sank with a gurgling sound.

"Where's my truck?" Claudia yelled. "I can't see it." She peered into the water where the truck had been.

"It sank while we were pulling you out," Jenny answered.

"I didn't know the creek was that deep," Calvin said.

"My dad's going to kill me! I am so-oo dead." Claudia sat on the bank and started to cry. The tears slid down her cheeks making clean lines through the muddy residue on her face. She pushed her wet hair out of her eyes. Her white shorts were covered with brown mud stains and her sneakers were filled with water.

"Can we do something?" Jenny asked.

"I guess you could tell my mom. She's at home."

"I'll go," Calvin offered, getting on his bike.

"Thanks," Claudia said tearfully. "Be sure to tell her that I'm all right."

"Okay. Will do," he answered with a salute. He rode up the path toward Claudia's house.

"I'll never be able to drive again," Claudia moaned. "Dad will be furious."

"He'll probably be happy you weren't hurt," Jenny said. She was happy that Claudia wasn't hurt. Jenny wouldn't have known what to do if Claudia had sunk with the truck.

"Maybe, but then he'll kill me." She put her head on her propped-up knees and cried softly. Jenny put her arm around Claudia, trying to comfort her.

A woman's voice called through the trees. "Claudia! Claudia!"

Claudia looked up. Her mom was running toward her. "Oh, Mom. I'm sorry." She burst into fresh tears.

"Are you all right?" Mrs. Livingston asked.

"Yes, but the truck sank." Claudia wiped the tears from her cheeks with the back of her muddy hands, smearing the tear stains.

"Sank?" Mrs. Livingston asked. "What do you mean sank?"

"I drove it into the creek!" Claudia wailed.

"What?" Mrs. Livingston couldn't believe what she heard. All Calvin told her was that Claudia had been in an accident. She rushed out the door before Calvin could give her any details.

"I was changing my CD," Claudia explained, "and I veered off the side of the road on the right. When I turned the steering wheel to get back on the road, I guess I turned it too much. The next thing I knew, I was on the other side of the road, bouncing up and down, heading for the creek."

"Oh, Claudia!" her mom cried, hugging her tightly. "I'm just glad you're alive. You could have drowned."

"I know, Mom." Claudia burst forth with a fresh batch of tears. She put her head on Mrs. Livingston's shoulder.

"We need to get you home and out of these wet clothes. You know we'll have to call Daddy about this," she said, leading Claudia up the bank with her arm around her shoulders. Mrs. Livingston looked back and told Jenny and Calvin, "Thank you both for helping Claudia."

"Your welcome," Calvin said.

"Whew," Jenny said. "I think I can breathe now."

"I know what you mean. Let's go home," Calvin said as he picked up the lunch. "I don't feel much like eating now."

"Neither do I," Jenny answered. She was anxious to go home and tell Argo and Marylou about Claudia.

Chapter Four

Another School Year Starts

The following Tuesday morning, Jenny and Calvin walked into Church Street Elementary School to check the class lists posted on the wall outside the office. They saw several of their friends checking the lists, also. Pete looked at his name and went down the hall without speaking to them. He looked sad.

Jenny ran her finger down the fourth grade lists. "Oh, no!"

"What? What's wrong?" Calvin asked.

Jenny turned to him. "We both have Miss Means!"

"No way," Calvin said. "Don't even joke about that."

"Look for yourself," Jenny said pointing to one list. "I kid you not."

"Oh, great," Calvin said. "This is going to be an awful year. At least you'll be in there with me."

"Thanks a lot," Jenny said sarcastically. "Some friend you are."

"I didn't mean it like that," Calvin tried to explain.

"Sure, sure," Jenny said with a sigh. "I guess we have to face the music." She walked down the hall toward Room 119. Halfway down the hall, Jenny poked Calvin and said, "Look!" She pointed to Miss Means standing at the door with her arms crossed, looking stern.

When the students reached her room, Miss Means said, "Go in and sit down, children. Your name is on your desk."

Jenny and Calvin slipped in the door, trying to stay as far away from Miss Means as they could. They found their desks. Jenny's desk was directly behind Calvin's. Once seated, Jenny leaned up toward Calvin and whispered, "Did you see her long fingernails? She looks like she could really claw someone."

"Quiet!" Miss Means said sternly. "There will be no talking in this class." She threw her hand in the air and pointed to Jenny.

Jenny and Calvin both jumped. They watched her head go back and forth and her hand bend in a strange way when she threw it into the air.

Now I know she's a witch, Jenny thought. She moves just like the witch in 'The Wizard of Oz'.

Later, out on the playground, Calvin ran over and stood beside Jenny. "Did you see how she ripped up Pete's paper, just because he didn't put his name in the right place?"

"Yeah," Jenny answered. "Did you hear her laugh when Mrs. Sunnyfield came into the room? It sounded just like a cackle."

"Yeah, like a witch's cackle," Calvin agreed.

"What are we going to do?" Jenny was worried about spending the whole school year with such an ill-tempered teacher.

"Let's have our parents come to the school and change us to Mrs. Sunnyfield's room," Calvin suggested.

"Can we do that?" Jenny asked. She looked hopeful.

"Ramon Rodriguez transferred from Mrs. Paul's room to Mrs. Smith's room last year," Calvin said.

"Yes, but Mrs. Paul isn't a witch," Jenny said. "I think Ramon moved because Mrs. Smith had the chorus students."

"Oh," Calvin said quietly.

"Let's talk to our parents, anyway," Jenny said. "It won't hurt."

"Okay." He walked toward the line their class was forming by Miss Means.

In class after lunch, Jenny and Calvin sat quietly, hardly daring to move. They did their assignments without asking questions or going up to Miss Means' desk. After school they ran home and sat in Jenny's kitchen. They were eating fresh-baked chocolate cookies that Argo had stacked up on a plate. "Argo, do you think Dad could get me transferred to another room at school?"

"Why?" Argo asked. She continued to stand at the kitchen sink peeling potatoes.

"Our teacher's a witch," Jenny said, as she took a big bite of cookie.

"What?" Argo dropped the potato peeler and spun around to face Jenny.

"An honest to goodness witch," Calvin said. "She has a long nose, long stringy hair, she cackles, long…"

"Wait a minute," Argo said. "Do you mean you've come to this conclusion from just one day in her class?"

"No, we knew it before today," Jenny said. "We were just hoping that we wouldn't be in her room."

"Has she told you she's a witch?" Argo asked.

"Well…no," Jenny said.

"Does she wave a wand and turn children into frogs?" Argo asked.

"No." Jenny giggled.

"Does she ride a broom to school?"

"Of course not!"

"Does she cast spells and make people do strange things?" Argo asked.

"I don't think so," Jenny said, "at least, I mean, I haven't seen her do anything like that."

"Jenny Jenkins!" Argo exclaimed. "Haven't I taught you in the last seven years that I've been your nanny, that you shouldn't judge people by how they look?"

"It's not just how she looks," Jenny said, shaking her finger. "She yells and acts mean, too."

"Maybe she has a reason," Argo said.

"A reason?" Jenny asked. Her eyebrows scrunched together.

"Yes," Argo answered. "Maybe she's unhappy, or feels bad, or is nervous about something."

"Well…" Jenny didn't know what to say.

"Just give her a chance," Argo said. "Give her a week. She may not be so bad after all."

"We could all be dead in a week!" Jenny said loudly.

"Oh, come on," Argo said. "Don't exaggerate. She can't be as bad as all that. The school wouldn't keep her if she were that bad. Please, just give it a try."

"Oh, all right," Jenny reluctantly agreed. "I'll try, if Calvin tries."

"I guess I could," Calvin said quietly, "if you try."

The first week was bad, but not as bad as Jenny and Calvin thought it would be. At the end of the week, on Friday the thirteenth, Miss Means had a substitute.

"Do you realize what day this is?" Jenny asked Calvin at recess.

"Yeah, it's Friday," Calvin answered. "Tomorrow I'm going fishing with my dad."

"Not just any Friday. It's Friday the thirteenth!"

"So?" Calvin looked confused.

"So, Miss Means is absent," Jenny told him. "She's probably off planning some witchery with candles and spells and stuff with black cats. Witches do those things on Friday the thirteenth," she said with authority.

"I didn't think of that." Calvin slapped his forehead with the palm of his hand.

"What can we do?" Jenny asked.

"We can't do anything," Calvin said.

"You're right," Jenny agreed. "I guess we just have to wait until she comes back to school and see what she's like then."

On Monday and Tuesday, Jenny and Calvin had the same substitute teacher. On Wednesday, Miss Means was back, only now, to the students' surprise, she was smiling. She stood in front of the class and said, "Class, I have a surprise for you. For the rest of the year, you'll have a teacher by the name of Mrs. Sweet."

The whole class clapped. Miss Means looked sad.

"Where are you going?" Jenny bravely asked.

"I'm not going anywhere. I meant to say that I got married and changed my name."

"Got married?" Jenny's mouth gaped open. She couldn't imagine who would want to marry Miss Means.

"Yes, last Saturday," she answered.

Jenny smiled and said, "We're happy for you, Miss Means."

"That's not my name anymore. I married a man named Steven Sweet. So, my new name is Mrs. Sweet."

"I like that name much better, Miss Means. Oops!" Jenny put her hand to her mouth. "I mean Mrs. Sweet." Several students giggled.

"I know that I may have been as mean as my name when school started," Mrs. Sweet told the class. Steven proposed to me on Labor Day. I had less than two weeks to plan our wedding. I was so nervous and upset that everything might not go right. Some days I even forgot to comb my hair."

"We were scared of you," Jenny admitted.

"I'm sorry." Mrs. Sweet looked unhappy. "I really didn't mean to scare anyone. What if we forget those first days and start all over again?"

"What do you mean?" Calvin asked.

"Let's pretend that this is the first day of school and start over."

"Okay," Calvin said happily. He high-fived Pete, who sat across from him.

43

"Hello, class. My name is Mrs. Sweet. I'm going to be your fourth grade teacher this year."

"Hello, Mrs. Sweet," the class chorused happily.

"I'm sure we're going to work together beautifully this year," Mrs. Sweet said.

"Yes, Mrs. Sweet," the class chorused.

After school, Jenny and Calvin couldn't wait to get home to tell their families about the change of events in their classroom. "I sure was wrong about Miss Means…I mean Mrs. Sweet," Jenny said to Calvin.

"So was everyone else," Calvin told her. "I'm glad things have changed. It sure was hard to keep my mind on math, when I was worried that I might be turned into a frog, or something."

"I know what you mean," Jenny said. She broke into a run when they rounded the corner and saw their houses. She ran the rest of the way home with her brown ponytail flying out behind her head like a flag, and her backpack bouncing on her back. Calvin ran at her side, anxious to be home and relate the events of the day.

Chapter Five
Good-by, Uncle Paul

———— ❦ ————

"Jenny, you didn't eat any of your breakfast," Argo said, frowning. "Isn't your stomach any better?"

"I just don't feel like eating," Jenny told her. She fell back on her pillow. "It's *so-oo boring* being sick." She stared at the ceiling and asked, "Do I still have a fever? If I don't, can I go downstairs?"

Argo felt Jenny's head. She said, "Your head is still hot. I'll bring you some Tylenol. That should help. If you feel better this afternoon, you can come down and lie on the sofa." Argo left the bedroom with the uneaten breakfast.

Jenny looked at the clock. It was only ten-thirty. She thought that if she were in school, she'd be in art class painting her mask green. Her class had made paper mache masks last week, and this week they were going to paint them.

Jenny surfed the channels on her television set. She found nothing interesting. The soap operas were boring, and she'd seen all the cartoons, The Disney Channel was showing 'Old Yeller,' which she'd already seen three times The talk show was about teen-age dads, which she thought was stupid. She would like to talk to Calvin, but he was in school. She'd read both of her library books, and she didn't really feel well enough to work on the big jigsaw puzzle on the dining room table, even if Argo would let her go downstairs while she still had a fever.

"Here's your Tylenol," Argo said. She came back into the room with two capsules and a glass of water.

"Is Uncle Paul awake?" Jenny asked.

"I don't think so," Argo answered. "I haven't heard anything from his room since he came in early this morning."

"He could be reading," Jenny said.

"Yes, but if you go into his room, don't get too near him. You don't want him to catch whatever it is that you have," Argo said. She turned and walked out of the room.

"Okay," Jenny said. She put her ear to the wall, listening for sounds from her uncle's room. Even though she heard nothing, she decided to investigate anyway. She slipped out of bed, stuck her feet into her gray kitty slippers, tiptoed down the hallway, and knocked softly on Uncle Paul's bedroom door.

"Uncle Paul," she called softly, "are you awake?" Hearing nothing, Jenny cracked open the door. "Whew!" Jenny said. She wrinkled her nose and waved her hand in front of her face. "Your room sure smells like cigarette smoke." She smelled another burnt smell, also, one that she couldn't identify.

Uncle Paul smoked heavily. Jenny told him often about the dangers of cigarettes, things she had learned in health class. Despite her warnings, he continued to smoke almost two packs of unfiltered cigarettes a day.

"Uncle Paul, are you awake?" Jenny asked again. She opened the door a little more. The dresser was blocking her view, so she could only see his feet when she peeked in. They were very, very still. Tiptoeing, Jenny crept into the room. Uncle Paul wasn't moving. Her eyes were drawn to his face. What she saw made her quickly cover her mouth with her hands to muffle the scream that came from her throat, for Uncle Paul's face was frozen in a death-like mask, as if he were screaming, or in extreme pain. His mouth was open, and his lips were pulled back from his teeth. He looked like one of those awful masks Calvin liked to wear on Halloween.

"Oh, Uncle Paul," Jenny whispered softly. "What happened?" She looked away from his face. Her eyes fell on the hand that stuck out from under the sheet. His fingers were red where he was holding a completely burned-down cigarette. She knew he was dead. His eyes were open just like the dead guys on TV. She wondered how long he'd been like this, right there next to her room.

Jenny stood in the middle of the room, not daring to move, not daring to breathe. Her mind whirled. Her thoughts spun around and around. She didn't know what to do. She knew that if she screamed and ran downstairs, Argo would scream, run upstairs, scream some more, call 911, and there would be thirty people in the house in five minutes.

Jenny loved Argo. Argo had taken care of her since her mother died in a car accident. But she did get very loud and upset at the smallest things. Jenny didn't know what Argo would do if she had to deal with a dead body.

Jenny felt dizzy. Her head felt hot. Her knees turned to jelly. She knew then that she did not want to deal with a loud, screaming Argo, policemen, paramedics, or anyone else right now. She turned and ran out of the room, closing the door quietly behind her. She ran down the hallway and into her room. She trembled and shook. She plopped on her bed, still wearing her kitty slippers, and covered up, in an attempt to stop shaking.

"Are you all right?" Argo called from the bottom of the stairs. "I heard you running."

"I was cold," Jenny called. "I ran to cover up."

"You're probably cold because of your fever," Argo called. "Stay covered up. Do you need anything?"

"No," Jenny called back. She didn't want Argo to come upstairs.

"Well, stay in bed. You'll get well faster."

"Okay," Jenny answered. Still shaking, she thought of what she could do. She could tell Argo and deal with the noise and confusion that would bring. She could call her dad at work and tell him what happened, but Argo would probably overhear her call, get upset, and start screaming. She could call 911, but Argo would still overhear her. Besides, if the paramedics came, they wouldn't be able to help Uncle Paul. He was dead. No one could help him. The last thing she could think of was to wait until her dad came home and let him deal with it. He'd be calm and do what had to be done, without getting as frantic as Argo would.

Jenny looked at the clock. It was eleven o'clock. Her dad wouldn't be home until five-thirty. She wondered if she could wait that long. She decided that she would rather wait, than tell Argo and deal with her hysteria. She pulled the covers up tightly against her neck. She knew that choosing this way was a cop-out, but after all, she reasoned to herself, she was only nine years old. Adults needed to deal with these things, not kids.

Jenny was almost asleep when Argo came into the room carrying a tray. "Jenny, I brought you some chicken noodle soup. Please try to eat some. It'll give you strength. She put the tray down beside Jenny on the little play table Jenny had used when she was younger. Argo brought it down from the attic for Jenny to use while she was sick. She leaned over and put her hand on Jenny's forehead. She smiled and said, "You feel much cooler. That's a good sign."

After Argo left the room, Jenny tasted the soup. She made a face by wrinkling up her nose. She pushed the tray away from her and fell back on the pillow. She thought of what she knew that no one else in the world knew. She knew she was strong, but this burden was almost too much, even for Jenny.

After a while, Argo came back into the room. "You didn't eat," she said.

"I wasn't hungry." Jenny put her hand on her stomach.

"You've got to eat," Argo said. "You need strength to get well."

"Maybe tonight," Jenny said. "I'm just not hungry now."

"Is your stomach still upset?" Argo asked.

"Yes, a little," Jenny answered, knowing that she was upset all over. She wanted to tell Argo about

Uncle Paul, but she didn't want to get her upset either. She still didn't feel well enough to deal with that.

Jenny stayed in bed all afternoon. She fell asleep once and dreamed an awful dream about her father dying. She woke up shaking. She wondered what would happen to her and Marylou, if that happened. Where would they go? Who would they live with? She hardly knew her aunts and uncles on her mother's side, except for Aunt Gertie. Everyone on her dad's side, except for her dad, now, was dead or lived in Sweden. She had never met any of them. A tear slid down her cheek to her lips. It tasted salty.

"I'm home," Marylou announced as she came in the front door.

Argo called from the kitchen, "I've just made some chocolate chip cookies. They're still warm."

After grabbing some cookies and pouring herself some milk, Marylou ran up the stairs and poked her head into Jenny's room. "Did you have fun skipping school?" she asked.

"I didn't skip school," Jenny said. "I'm sick."

"Sure you are," Marylou answered. "If you skip in middle school, you get put in ISS. You'd better remember that."

"What's ISS?" Jenny asked.

"In School Suspension, dummy," Marylou said as she walked off toward her room.

"I'm sick, and I didn't skip," Jenny called to Marylou's back.

"Sure you didn't," Marylou answered in a smart-aleck tone.

If she wasn't so mean, I'd tell her about Uncle Paul, Jenny thought to herself.

No one thought too much about not seeing Uncle Paul all day, because he usually slept until dinnertime. Jenny's dad would wake him and tell him that dinner was ready, then, after dinner, Uncle Paul would visit with the family until it was time to go to work.

Jenny tried to pass the time by watching some cartoons on television, before her dad came home. She looked at the clock when she heard his car in the driveway. He was right on time, five-thirty. She threw off her covers and sat up on the side of the bed. Her kitty slippers were still on her feet. She slid to the floor, walked to the top of the stairs, and sat down, waiting for her dad to come in the front door. As soon as he walked in, Jenny called, "Dad, can you come up here, right now?"

"What's the matter, honey?" Mr. Jenkins asked.

Unable to keep it in any longer, Jenny cried, "Uncle Paul is dead!"

"What!" he yelled, bounding up the stairs two at a time. He ran down the hallway, threw open Uncle Paul's bedroom door, leaped to the middle of the room, and stood, staring at his brother.

"Omigosh!" he yelled. He ran out of the room and into Jenny's room, where she sat on the bed, her feet dangling. He asked Jenny, "How long have you known? He's been dead a long time."

"I know," Jenny said. "I found him this morning."

"This morning?" Mr. Jenkins asked in a too loud voice. "Why didn't you tell Argo? Why didn't you call me?"

"What good would it have done? When I found him, he was already dead. Argo couldn't help him. You couldn't help him. No one could!" Jenny cried. Tears ran down her cheeks.

Mr. Jenkins ran downstairs and told Argo and Marylou about Uncle Paul. Then he called 911, even though the paramedics couldn't help him. He didn't know who else to call. He told the dispatcher what had happened and gave her the address.

Argo yelled, "Oh, no! How did it happen? Are you sure he's dead?"

Marylou cried, "I was so mean to him. Did he die because I was mean?"

Mr. Jenkins calmed them both down by talking softly and gently. He made them both sit down on the sofa, before he told them, "Yes, I'm very sure that he's dead. No, he didn't die because you were mean. He probably had a heart attack. He did smoke non-filtered cigarettes against his doctor's wishes."

Sirens screamed down the street. Emergency vehicles screeched to a stop in front of the big yellow house. Policemen, fireman, and paramedics ran up the walkway, and someone pounded on the door.

"Come in," Mr. Jenkins said in a flat voice, as he opened the door. "My brother is upstairs on the left."

"What happened?" a policeman asked.

"My daughter found my brother dead this morning, and…"

"This morning!" the policeman yelled. "Why did we just get the call?"

"She didn't know what to do," Mr. Jenkins explained.

"That's incredible," the policeman said. "Most people wouldn't keep something like that to themselves, especially a child."

The paramedics slowly descended the steps with Uncle Paul on a stretcher. Over the day, his body had stiffened, so the paramedics couldn't lay him flat on the stretcher. Jenny noticed that the white sheet poked up where his hand stuck up, the one that held the cigarette.

"We have to take him in for an autopsy," the shorter paramedic explained to Mr. Jenkins. "It's the law in Summerville. You'll be called when the body can be released to a funeral home."

Jenny was exhausted from everything that had happened, especially from keeping such a secret to herself for most of the day. She slowly walked up the stairs and into her room. She fell back on her bed; the events of the day swirled around and around in her head. "Poor Uncle Paul," she thought out loud. "I wonder if I could have done anything, if I had gone in sooner."

Overhearing his daughter, Mr. Jenkins came in and sat on Jenny's bed. He put his arm around her shoulders and hugged her close. "No, you couldn't have done anything. From the looks of him, he probably died instantly. Why didn't you call me when you found him?"

"I felt sick," Jenny said. Argo would have heard me. She would have screamed and yelled. I didn't feel well enough to hear that today." Jenny suddenly jerked away from her father. "Oh! What time is it?"

Mr. Jenkins looked at his watch. "It's almost seven o'clock. Why? What's so important about the time?"

"Uncle Paul is supposed to go to work tonight," Jenny said. "Someone should call the hotel."

"Good thinking," Mr. Jenkins said. "I'd forgotten about that, and they do need to know. "I'll call immediately." Mr. Jenkins left the room to use the phone in the hallway.

* * * * * * * *

At the funeral, Jenny sat in the front row between Marylou and Argo. She kept her eyes on Uncle Paul in the casket. She wanted him to be alive, sit up and climb out, saying that there had been a big mistake. She didn't want to believe that he was actually dead.

"He looks so peaceful," Jenny thought aloud.

"Hush," Argo said softly.

"Is he really dead?" Jenny asked.

"Yes, sweetheart, he is," Argo said. She put her arm around Jenny.

The minister led the service for Uncle Paul, telling about his life and the family he left behind, but Jenny didn't listen to what he said. She only thought of the wonderful times she had with Uncle Paul and how much she would miss him.

"Good-by," Uncle Paul," Jenny whispered. "I'll miss you." A single tear ran down her cheek and dropped on her hand. Jenny knew that she would never forget her uncle.

Chapter Six

Help! The Dog's in the Tree!

"Mom, what can I do to make Jenny happy?" Calvin asked at breakfast, two days after Uncle Paul's funeral. "She's been so sad since her uncle died."

"You could help get her mind on something else," Mrs. Kelly said.

"What do you mean?" Calvin asked.

"Well, didn't you teach Buffy a new trick?" Mrs. Kelly referred to Calvin's dog, a golden cocker spaniel.

"Yeah, I did," Calvin said brightly.

"Well, you could show Jenny the trick," Mrs. Kelly said. "It might get her mind off her sadness. It might even make her laugh."

"Thanks, Mom!" Calvin said. He ran out onto the front porch and down the steps. He found his dog lying in the shade of the magnolia tree. He yelled, "Come on, Buffy! Let's go!"

Buffy, hearing her name, jerked up her head, jumped up, and ran after Calvin.

Calvin grabbed the five-foot stepladder, which was leaning against the side of the garage and dragged it across his yard and into Jenny's. He set it up on the walkway leading to her front door, ran up the porch steps, and rang the doorbell.

"Just a minute," Argo called. She came to the door wiping flour from her hands on her apron. "Hi, Calvin," she said as she opened the door. "Come on in."

"Can Jenny come out?" Calvin asked. "I've got something to show her."

"She's upstairs. I'll see what she wants to do." Argo turned toward the stairway and called, "Jenny, Calvin's here. He has something to show you."

"I'm coming," Jenny called back from her room.

"Can you come out?" Calvin asked, as Jenny ran down the stairs. "Buffy learned a new trick."

"What kind of trick?" Jenny asked with interest. She banged open the screen door and ran down the porch steps, her long, brown ponytail flying out behind her. They ran out into the yard where Buffy stood, wagging her whole back end, beside the stepladder. She barked a greeting as they ran toward her. Buffy sat down when Jenny rubbed her head.

"Why is there a ladder out here?" Jenny asked. "Is it yours?"

"That's Buffy's new trick," Calvin said.

"The ladder is Buffy's trick?" Jenny looked confused.

"Not just the ladder," Calvin told her. "Buffy can climb it."

"No way!" Jenny said. "Dogs can't climb ladders."

"Buffy can. Watch." Calvin whistled and pointed up the ladder. Buffy stood up, ran to the ladder, and put her two front paws on the second step. She then put one hind paw on the first step, followed by the second hind paw. She then moved her front paws up one step, with her hind paws following, one at a time, until she was sitting on the top, wiggling her tail and barking.

"She looks so funny up there," Jenny said, laughing. "Can she come down by herself, or do you have to help her?"

"Watch." Calvin whistled again. Buffy put her front paws on the first step down, then put one hind leg on the step where her front paws were. She moved her front legs to the next step and moved the next hind leg down to join the other. She repeated these motions until she was on the ground. She sat in front of Calvin, wiggling her tail, and waiting for him to pet her and tell her that she was a good dog.

"Awesome!" Jenny exclaimed. "Let's show Argo." She ran up the porch steps and called, "Argo, come here. You've just got to see this."

Argo came to the doorway. She smiled as she watched Buffy repeat her performance. "You've got a talented dog, Calvin. You should take a video and send it to one of those funniest home video shows on television. You might make some money."

"Cool!" he said, grinning. "I'd be famous, too."

After Argo went back into the kitchen, Jenny glanced at the big oak tree in her front yard. It had two large main branches coming out of a massive trunk. Between the two branches was a large flat area that looked like a seat. "Look, Calvin. The ladder is about the same height as the fork in the tree."

"So?" Calvin asked.

"So, we could put the ladder by the tree and climb into it," Jenny said. "I've always wanted to climb that tree, but I never could get up the big trunk."

"Cool!" Calvin exclaimed.

Together, they carried the ladder over to the tree and set it next to the fork on the side away from the house. Jenny didn't want Argo to look out the window and see them. She would tell Jenny not to go up, because she might get hurt. Jenny remembered the time when she was four and Argo freaked out when she had climbed the cherry tree to pick cherries. Jenny scrambled up the ladder first and stepped off into the tree. She climbed up the large sloping branch that went in the direction of her house and looked into her father's bedroom window. "This is so cool!" she exclaimed.

Calvin, not to be outdone by Jenny, also scrambled up the ladder and into the tree. He climbed up the branch that went in the direction of the street. "Awesome!" he said. "I can see a truck coming all the way down by the store. Look! There's Claudia riding her bike, with her big black dog tied to her handlebars. I guess she doesn't have her truck back yet."

"I can't see from here," Jenny complained. She came down her branch and climbed up Calvin's. "Look! There's Mrs. Johnson walking the twins," she said. "I feel like a spy. We can see people, but they can't see us. I've never been this high in a tree before."

"Neither have I," Calvin said, grinning at Jenny. "This is fun."

"I hope Argo doesn't see us," Jenny said. "She'll get upset and tell us that we're going to get hurt, then make us go down."

Jenny and Calvin were having so much fun, climbing higher and higher, that they forgot about Buffy. Jenny hummed and Calvin whistled. Hearing her master's whistle, Buffy scrambled up the ladder.

"Look!" Jenny cried. "We're higher than the house!"

In her excitement of climbing the ladder and hearing the squeal of Jenny's voice, Buffy jumped off the ladder and into the fork of the tree. She jumped with such force, that her hind feet pushed the ladder. It fell to the ground with a clatter.

"Oh, no!" Calvin yelled. "How are we going to get down?"

Buffy barked wildly attracting a lot of attention. Mrs. Johnson walked closer and peered up into the tree. She said, "Look, boys. There's a dog barking in the tree."

"How did it get up there?" Mark, one of the twins, asked.

"Why is it up there?" David, the other twin, asked. "Can it get down?"

"Dogs can't climb trees," Mark said.

"This one did," David told his brother with authority in his voice.

"Mrs. Johnson," Jenny called. "Can you help us?"

Mrs. Johnson peered into the tree with her hand held above her eyes for a sunshade. "Why, Jenny, what are you doing up there? You're going to get hurt. What if you fall?" Jenny thought she sounded like Argo.

Buffy barked louder than ever.

"Mrs. Johnson," Jenny repeated. "Can you help...?" Jenny said, as her voice was drowned out by Buffy's barking.

At that moment, a city bus rumbled down the street. Mrs. Davis, the fat lady who sang in the church choir, sat by an open window behind the driver. Seeing Buffy, she leaned out of the window. Her large arms waved, and her ample chest hung down the outside of the window. "Look!" she screamed. "There's a dog in the tree!"

Startled by the scream behind him, Mr. Adams, the bus driver, looked. He took his eyes off the road and stared at Buffy, who barked in the tree. Glancing back out the windshield, he yelled, "Oh, no!"

"Oh, no!" Mrs. Johnson yelled.

"Oh, my goodness!" Jenny yelled.

"Look!" Calvin yelled.

The bus jumped the curb on the other side of the street and headed straight toward a fire hydrant. "Someone! Anyone!" Mrs. Davis yelled. "Do something! Help!"

Crash. Crunch. The bus hit the fire hydrant. Swoosh. A geyser of water shot straight up into the air, spurting high above the bus.

"Awesome!" Calvin yelled.

"Help!" Mrs. Davis screamed again, as water streamed down from the top of the bus and onto her head. Her hair was plastered to her face. Her wet dress stuck to her large chest.

"There, there, Mrs. Davis. Are you hurt?" Mr. Adams asked, as he patted her on the back.

Argo, hearing all the commotion, looked out of the dining room window. "Oh, my goodness!" she yelled. She ran out the front door, down the steps, and into the yard, waving a dishtowel.

"Hi, Argo," Jenny called from the tree.

Holding her hands to her chest, forgetting about the bus, Argo screamed, "Help! Jenny's too high in the tree. She'll fall. Someone, please help!"

Calvin's mother heard the crash and all the screaming. She ran over from her back yard, still holding the trowel she was using to plant pansies. "What's going on?" she asked.

Argo waved her arms wildly and tried to point into the tree. She gasped, "Look!"

"Hi, Mom," Calvin said brightly.

Mrs. Kelly looked up. "Calvin," she said sternly. "What are you doing up there? Come down before you get hurt," she ordered.

Argo waved her dishtowel and yelled, "I'm calling 911!" She spun around and ran up the steps and into the house. The last time Jenny had seen Argo move that fast was when she was four and had climbed into the cherry tree.

"Mom, if you put up the ladder, we can get down," Calvin told Mrs. Kelly.

"Ladder? What ladder?" Mrs. Kelly asked.

"It's on the other side of the tree, Mrs. Kelly," Jenny said, pointing down towards the ladder.

"Oh. Okay," she said. Mrs. Kelly walked over and picked up the ladder. She set it up beside the tree. "I can see how you two can get down, but what about Buffy?"

"If you whistle, she'll go down," Calvin told her.

Mrs. Kelly whistled. Buffy stopped barking and looked at Mrs. Kelly. Then she stepped over onto the top of the ladder. Putting one paw after another, she slowly climbed down, one step at a time. She jumped the last two steps to the ground, ran over and sat by Mrs. Kelly's feet, wiggling her tail and waiting for Mrs. Kelly to praise her.

Jenny and Calvin climbed down. Two police cars, one fire truck, and an ambulance screamed down the street, all screeching to a stop in front of the Jenkins' house. A tall, blonde policeman ran up to Mrs. Kelly. "Is anyone hurt over here, Ma-am?"

"Everyone's fine," she said. "We weren't on the bus."

The policemen, the firemen, and the paramedics ran over to the bus. Argo came out of the house and said, "I called your dad, too. He's on his way home."

"Relax, Argo. We're down," Jenny and Calvin chorused.

Upon hearing that, Argo rushed over to the ladder, grabbed it, and shoved it toward Mrs. Kelly. "Please take this home and lock it in your garage," she said. "I don't want the children to use it to climb into the tree again. I worry that they might fall and get hurt. Calvin's tree house is much closer to the ground than the big old oak branches." Turning toward Jenny and Calvin, she shouted, "You will never, never do anything like that again! Look what you caused!" She waved her hand toward the wrecked bus, its soaked passengers, the water geyser, the policemen, the firemen, and the paramedics. Turning around, Argo marched back into the house, her black hair streaming down from the doughnut-like bun she wore at the back of her head. Her face was red. Beads of perspiration were dotted all over her forehead.

"We may as well stay and watch the show," Mrs. Kelly said. She sat down on the grass and watched the activities of the policemen and firemen. Everyone was soaked.

The firemen tried to stop the water from spurting, the paramedics tried to calm Mrs. Davis down, and the policemen directed traffic and asked a lot of questions.

Jenny sighed, as she plopped down on the ground, snuggling her back against the tree. "What a day!"

"Yeah," Calvin agreed. "Let's keep Buffy away from ladders." He plopped down beside her.

"No one seems to be hurt," Mrs. Kelly said. "That's good."

"Things could have been worse," Calvin said with relief. "Someone over there could be cut, or their leg broken, or…"

"What about over here?" Mrs. Kelly asked. "What about you, and Jenny, and Buffy? You were all quite high up. Any of you could have fallen and broken any part of you."

"Yeah," Calvin said as he hung his head. "I'm sorry, Mom."

"I'm sorry, too," Jenny said. "Maybe we could teach Buffy something safe, like roll over, play dead, or fetch."

"Nah," Calvin said. "Any dog can do that. We need to teach her something else, like how to walk on her hind legs."

"Cool!" Jenny said.

Excited, Jenny and Calvin both jumped up to find Buffy. They couldn't find her anywhere outside, so they crawled through the doggy door on Calvin's back porch and found her sleeping in her bed in the kitchen,

"She's sleeping," Jenny whispered. "We must have worn her out."

"Oh, well. Let's try it tomorrow," Calvin said. They turned and ran out of his house. "I think I've had enough excitement for one day."

"Me, too," Jenny sighed. "Let's ride down to the store for ice cream."

"Okay. Let's go," Calvin answered. He grabbed his bike and thought that Jenny didn't seem so sad anymore. It was worth getting yelled at, he thought, if Jenny forgot her sadness, even for a short time.

Chapter Seven

Clean Up

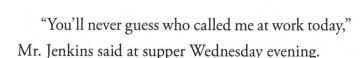

"You'll never guess who called me at work today," Mr. Jenkins said at supper Wednesday evening.

"Who, Daddy?" Jenny asked.

"Aunt Gertie."

"Aunt Gertie? She's weird."

"Jenny!" Argo said sharply.

"Well, she is. She juices everything. When I went to her house, she juiced potato peels and carrots, and then she made me drink a glass of the stuff."

"Gross!" Marylou said, wrinkling her nose. "When I went there for a visit, we didn't eat any meat the whole weekend. Remember, Daddy?" Marylou looked at Mr. Jenkins. "I had you stop and get some chicken on the way home."

"I remember, sweetheart," Mr. Jenkins answered, smiling. "You pestered me until I stopped. You said that you would die if you didn't eat some meat before we got home."

"I probably would've," Marylou said.

"I didn't eat any meat when I went," Jenny told her. "I just thought she was out of groceries or something."

"She's a vegetarian," Mr. Jenkins said.

"A vege-what?" Jenny asked.

"A vegetarian," Mr. Jenkins said. "It refers to people who won't eat any meat."

"No hamburgers, or pepperoni, or ham, or....?" Jenny asked.

"No," Mr. Jenkins interrupted. "No meat of any kind."

"How can you live without meat?" Marylou asked. "I thought it was good for you."

"There's protein in meat. Protein is good for you, but you can get protein from other things like beans, cheese, and peanut butter. Some people think that it's healthier not to eat meat. Other people just don't want animals to die, just so they can eat," Mr. Jenkins answered.

"Why doesn't Aunt Gertie eat meat?" Marylou asked.

"She's a health nut," Mr. Jenkins said. "She doesn't like microwave ovens, white bread, sugar, or fried foods, either."

"No French fries? No chocolate cake?" Jenny asked.

"No."

"Why did she call?" Argo asked.

"She wants to come for a visit," Mr. Jenkins told her.

"A visit? Here?" Jenny asked.

"Yes, here," Mr. Jenkins answered.

"What will she eat if she doesn't like this stuff?" Jenny asked, pointing to a table full of fried chicken, fried okra, white dinner rolls, and German chocolate cake.

"She's only going to stay for a few days. I'm sure we'll survive if we do without some of this kind of food for a few days." Mr. Jenkins patted Jenny on the shoulder.

"I won't," Marylou complained sticking her lower lip out.

"Sure you will," Argo said. "Besides, if you do eat the food she disapproves of, she'll let us know about it. She'll lecture us on our bad food habits and tell us about all the things that she thinks will happen to us if we eat them. Personally, I would rather humor her for a short visit than listen to her lectures." Argo looked at Mr. Jenkins and asked, "When is she coming?"

"Next Thursday. Why?"

"I need to clean up and paint Paul's room. Will you go to the Mattress Factory after work tomorrow and buy a new mattress and box springs for the bed?" Argo asked.

"Sure, but I won't be home until around six-thirty, if I do."

"I'll buy some paint at Home Mart tomorrow, when I go out for groceries. How long did you say she was staying?"

"I didn't say, but she wants to stay five or six days," Mr. Jenkins said.

"Gertie said that she wants to get to know the girls better. She misses her sister and wants to know her sister's children better than she does now."

"Five or six days! I'll never survive!" Marylou complained. "Can I stay with Lisa while she's here?"

"Yes you will, and no, you can't," Argo told her sternly. "Besides, she does have a good sense of humor, so it should be an interesting visit. I just hope she keeps her animals at home."

"I don't!" Jenny exclaimed, happily. She popped a large piece of German chocolate cake in her mouth and grinned.

* * * * * * * *

The next morning, even before Jenny and Marylou went to school, Argo was packing up Uncle Paul's clothes in cardboard boxes. "I called The Salvation Army this morning, and they're sending a truck tomorrow for Paul's clothes," she told the girls as she took a break from packing and put cereal and toast on the table. "That's quick service! I'm glad they'll take them. I'd hate to just throw them away. If there's anything you girls want, you need to tell me now, or get it before you go to school.

"I want to keep that porcelain cat he kept on his dresser," Jenny said.

"I want that fuzzy blue sweater that he let me wear sometimes," Marylou said.

"I'll keep those things out, along with his pictures and some papers that your dad needs to go through. By the way, when I was cleaning out his sock drawer, I found six hundred dollars under the drawer liner. I'm sure that he'd want you girls to have it, so I'll open a savings account for each of you with half of the money. You can buy something someday in his memory, or use it for college."

"Thanks, Argo," Jenny and Marylou said together.

Argo would never think about keeping the money. She loved the girls and was always fair, treating each of them equally.

"I'm going to Home Mart while I'm out today," Argo told them. "I plan to pick up paint, new curtains, and a bedspread. I'll probably be ready to paint on Saturday. Your dad is going to take the mattress and box springs out in the backyard. You can jump on them for a few days, if you like, before he burns them."

"Cool!" Jenny said.

"Why is he going to burn them?" Marylou asked. "Why not give them to Salvation Army?"

"They're very old," Argo replied. "The Salvation Army doesn't want them. Besides, no one would want to sleep on a mattress that someone died on."

"Oh." Marylou looked thoughtful. She didn't think she'd like to sleep on it, either.

On Friday, Argo filled up all the nail holes and sanded the chipped woodwork in Uncle Paul's room. She put all the furniture in the middle of the room and covered it with plastic sheeting. On Saturday, she was ready to paint.

"Jim, will you carry the ladder upstairs for me? Girls, after breakfast, will you go down in the basement and get the brushes, rollers, and the roller pan and bring it all upstairs? The paint is already there."

"Sure we will," Mr. Jenkins answered for all three of them. "If I didn't have to go into work this morning, I'd help you paint. I'll lend a hand when I get home."

"Thanks," Argo answered. "You girls will have to stay out from underfoot. I'd like to get the whole room painted today."

"I'm going to Lisa's house this morning," Marylou announced. She bought a new CD."

"May I watch, if I stay out of the way?" Jenny asked.

"Yes, but no running around in there," Argo said.

"Okay," Jenny agreed.

Later in Uncle Paul's bedroom, Jenny sat quietly against the doorway, while Argo climbed the ladder and painted up next to the ceiling on the opposite wall. "Why are you using such a little brush, Argo?" Jenny asked.

"I want to be careful not to paint on the ceiling."

"Oh. What's that? I think I hear somebody at the door. I'll get it,"

Jenny said as she jumped up and ran out of the bedroom. She ran down the stairs and jumped the last three steps. Calvin and Buffy, his dog, were at the door. "Hi, Calvin. Come on in. I want to show you how big the squirrels are now. They're almost as big as their mother. I've been feeding them pecan cookies from my window. They're so tame that they come and take the cookies right out of my hand."

"Cool!" Calvin exclaimed. "Do you think they'll let me feed them, too?"

"I don't know," Jenny said. "You can try."

Running upstairs, the children didn't notice that Buffy had followed Calvin inside and ran upstairs with them. As she passed the open bedroom door where Argo was standing on the ladder, she made a quick turn, ran into the bedroom, and climbed the ladder with Argo.

"Eeek! What's that?" Argo screamed loudly. Startled by the touch of Buffy's cold nose on her right leg, she screamed again. "Help!" She threw her hands into the air, which made her tip sideways. Still not knowing what was behind her, she screamed louder. "Help! It's attacking me! Help!"

"What's wrong, Argo?" Jenny called, running down the hallway.

"I'm being attacked! There's something wild in here with me!" Argo yelled, as the ladder fell sideways and landed against the stacked furniture. Argo, however, landed on the floor with the paint can sitting upside-down, at an angle, on her head.

"Oh, no!" Jenny yelled.

Calvin couldn't say anything.

"Just look at this mess!" Argo sputtered, wiping light blue paint from her right eye.

"Are you hurt?" Jenny asked, running over to her.

"I don't think so," Argo said, as she moved her arms and legs up and down, one at a time. "Nothing seems to be broken. What was that behind me?"

"Buffy went up the ladder with you," Calvin explained.

"Buffy? That was only Buffy?" Argo sputtered.

"Yeah," Calvin said quietly. He hung his head. "I guess she just misses climbing ladders."

"Well, Calvin Kelly, you can just get that dog out of here, right now! Look at the mess she made."

"I'm sorry," Calvin said.

"Well, being sorry isn't enough right now. Take that dog home, now. Then, I want the both of you to come back up here and clean up the spilled paint, while I take a shower." Argo marched heavily out of the bedroom.

"Oh, Buffy! We ought to make you clean it up. You did it." Calvin scolded, as he led Buffy down the stairs and out the door.

While Calvin was gone, Jenny ran to the broom closet, gathering up rags, a pail, and some lemon cleaner. Then, she poked her head in the cupboard under the kitchen sink and grabbed a new roll of paper towels and an old grocery bag. After filling the pail halfway with warm water and lemon cleaner, Jenny carried the bucket and the rest of the supplies upstairs.

"I'm back!" Calvin yelled at the door, just as Jenny reached the top step.

"Let yourself in and come upstairs," Jenny called. "I can use all the help I can get."

"Okay." Calvin swung open the screen door and ran up the stairs.

After walking into the paint-splattered bedroom, Jenny picked up the paint can and sighed. "This sure is a big mess. No wonder Argo was so mad," she said aloud. She unwound the whole roll of paper towels and laid them on the spilled paint to soak it up.

"What can I do?" Calvin asked as he walked into the room.

"First we need to soak up as much paint as we can. Then we need to scrub the floor with the soapy water. Hopefully, it will all come up," Jenny said, waving her hand at the spilled paint. "The mess is bigger than I first thought."

"Whew! This will take all day!" Calvin exclaimed as he turned over the paper towels to soak up more paint. "I chained Buffy up so she can't do any more damage."

"Good," Jenny answered, as she gathered up soaked paper towels and stuffed them into the grocery bag. They both wiped up as much as they could with the soapy water and the rags. "Look! The paint has gone down into the cracks in the wood. We can't get it all up."

Coming into the room, Argo stopped and took in the scene. "I think you're right, Jenny," she said, her voice much calmer than before. "I'll have to see if Home Mart has a big rug to put in here, when I pick up some more paint. I'll drive down there when your father gets home. I'm not going to paint any more until Monday." She looked at them both and finished saying, with her hands on her hips, "when you're both in school and the doors are locked." With that said, Argo turned and left the room.

"Whew! I thought she'd still be real mad," Calvin said, leaning against the wall. He wiped his forehead with the back of his hand.

"She usually doesn't stay mad," Jenny said. "Besides, she wanted to get a new rug for this room, anyway, but Dad didn't want to buy one. Now he has to. Maybe she's glad this happened."

"Maybe that's why she doesn't seem mad anymore," Calvin said."

"Well, whatever it is, I'm glad, too. Let's put this stuff away and go get Buffy off her chain. We can ride down to the park and play until things settle down here," Jenny suggested.

"Okay," Calvin said, following her. "Dad bought me a new fishing pole. I can try it out in the pond down there."

"We have some worms in the compost pile behind the garage. I'll put some in a pail and get my pole, too. I'll tell Argo and be right out."

Calvin ran toward his house while Jenny ran to ask Argo.

"Argo, I have a great idea that will get Calvin, Buffy, and me out of your hair for a while."

"I'm all ears, Jenny. What's this plan of yours?"

Jenny explained about the park as she grabbed a warm chocolate chip cookie from the cooling rack on the counter. "You need to eat something, or take it with you," Argo said. "It's almost time for lunch."

"Okay. I'll make some peanut butter sandwiches and grab a couple of Cokes from the fridge. If we catch some catfish, will you fry them for us?" Jenny asked, taking the peanut butter, bread, and grape jelly out of the cupboard.

"Sure," Argo answered, "if you or your dad cleans them.

"You're the best mom ever!" Jenny said. She ran over and hugged Argo around the waist.

Argo had tears in her eyes. Jenny had never called her 'Mom' before.

Jenny went back to the counter and spread thick layers of peanut butter and grape jelly on the bread, wrapped them in foil, and plopped them into a paper bag with the Cokes. "May we have some of your chocolate chip cookies, too?"

"Sure," Argo answered taking four large cookies from the cooling rack and wrapping them in foil. She put them in the bag on top of the sandwiches and folded the top of the bag over twice.

Jenny grabbed the bag, told Argo "Bye," ran out the kitchen door letting the screen door slam, and jumped down the porch steps.

"Where were you?" Calvin asked when he saw her.

"Making some sandwiches. Argo said we had to eat."

"Cool, I can always eat," Calvin said rubbing his stomach. "Did you get the worms yet?"

"No. Let's do it now," Jenny answered grabbing a pail that was sitting on the steps. She ran toward the compost pile, with Calvin on her heels. She dug in and was immediately rewarded with two shovels full of compost with dozens of fat, crawling worms. "This should be enough."

"I'll take the worm pail on my handlebars, if you carry the food in your basket," Calvin offered.

"Okay. I hope we catch some fish. Next weekend I won't be able to eat any fish or fried foods," she complained.

"Why?" Calvin asked as he threw his leg over his bike.

"My Aunt Gertie is coming. She won't eat meat, fish, fried foods. sugar…"

"Why?" Calvin looked confused.

"Dad says she's a health nut," Jenny answered, getting on her bike.

Calvin took off, and Jenny peddled as fast as she could after him. "My Uncle Max is like that," Calvin said when Jenny caught up to him. "Is she married? Maybe we should introduce them."

"If they get married, would we be related?" Jenny asked.

"I think so," Calvin answered. "At least, we would be able to go to the same weddings, family reunions, and things like that."

"What if your mom and my dad got married?" Jenny asked, as they approached the pond. "Then we would really be related." She hopped off her bike at the edge of the water. "That would be cool," Calvin replied, getting off his bike. "My mom and dad have been divorced for a long time. Dad married Julie last summer, so I know he won't come back to live with us."

"Maybe we could work on that," Jenny said. "It would be fun to have you for a brother."

"Why do people want to get married anyway?" Calvin asked.

"I don't know," Jenny answered.

"You know that when you get married you have to kiss."

"You have to?" Jenny asked in a loud voice.

"Yeah. It's a requirement," Calvin said with authority. "Anyway, haven't you ever been to a wedding? The lady and the man have to kiss to be married."

"Really? That's gross!" Jenny said, wrinkling her nose.

"Yeah, it is. But, when you're married you have to do a lot of gross stuff. Kissing is the worst, though."

"I'm never going to get married," Jenny said leaning back on her elbows, holding her fishing pole.

"Me, neither," Calvin answered. He put a fat, juicy worm on Jenny's hook, and then he put one on his. "I like my life just the way it is."

"Me, too," Jenny answered as she tossed her line in the water. "I wish I didn't have to grow up. I like being a kid."

Chapter Eight
Aunt Gertie

"Jenny! Marylou!" Argo called from the front door. "Come help me with this rug!"

Jenny and Marylou ran to the doorway, each with a glass of milk in one hand and a chocolate chip cookie in the other. "What do you want us to do?" Marylou asked. "Come help me carry this new rug. If you carry one end and Jenny carries the middle, the three of us ought to able to carry it out of the van and upstairs," she told them.

Jenny and Marylou shoved their cookies into their mouths and gulped down their milk. They ran out to the van and helped Argo tug and pull the big rug out of the back and off the two seats that it lay across.

"It's so heavy," Jenny said. "How did you get it in here?"

"Two men at Home Mart loaded it," Argo explained.

"Oh, look. The middle part is sagging with just me holding it," Jenny said. "It's too heavy. I'll run and get Calvin. He'll help." Jenny took off in a sprint across the yard. She rang the doorbell twice. When Mrs. Kelly came to the door, Jenny asked, "May Calvin come and help us carry a rug upstairs? It's too heavy for us."

"Of course. I'll get him. I'll help, too. After all, you wouldn't have had to buy a rug if it wasn't for our dog." She turned and called, "Calvin! Come here!"

"What's up?" he asked, running up from the basement, with a screwdriver in his hand.

"We're going to help Jenny carry a rug upstairs."`

"Okay." He put the screwdriver on the table by the front door.

Jenny, Calvin, and Mrs. Kelly walked over to the van, and the five of them picked up the rug that was lying on the lawn behind the van. "It's much easier to carry now," Jenny said.

"It's the least we can do," Mrs. Kelly answered. "I'm sorry you had to buy it because of Buffy's mess-up."

"I'm not," Argo answered, smiling. "I wanted to put one in that bedroom, but Jim didn't want to buy one. Because of the paint, he really didn't have much of a choice, other than sanding down the floor and refinishing the whole room."

Mrs. Kelly, leading the way, opened the front door. "Which way to the bedroom?"

"Up the stairs, to the left, and down the hall," Argo answered. "I'll try to hold this end up back here," she continued, as she pushed the door closed with her foot.

Once in the room, they laid the rug down in the middle of the floor, then put the furniture in place. "Whew! I'm glad that's over," Jenny sighed. She rubbed the back of her hand across her forehead.

"It's not over yet," Argo said. "Your Aunt Gertie arrives the day after tomorrow. There's still a lot of work to do."

"Like what?" Marylou asked.

"Well, we have to hide the microwave. The cake mixes, the sugar, the food with preservatives, and the soft drinks. The meat in the freezer needs to be put under the vegetables, and the sugar coated cereal needs to be put away."

"Why all the secrecy?" Mrs. Kelly asked.

"Gertie is a health nut," Argo told her, as they were walking back down the hall. "I'd rather put it all away than hear sermons about what these things can do to your health."

"Oh, look. One of the squirrels is looking in your window," Calvin said, pointing into Jenny's room. "Can we feed it some of your pecan cookies?"

"Help yourself," Jenny answered. "They're on the dresser."

"I've heard so much about these squirrels," Mrs. Kelly said to Argo. "Calvin has given me detailed descriptions. I almost feel like I know them."

"They are cute," Argo said, starting down the stairs. "I just hope they don't get back into the attic. Thanks for your help with the rug. I don't think we could have done it without you."

"We were glad to. Calvin would rather be working over here than playing at our house," Mrs. Kelly said, opening the front door. "Please send him home if he gets underfoot, or by six o'clock for dinner," she continued, heading down the porch steps and toward her house. She turned and waved.

Thursday afternoon, just as Jenny arrived home from school, a red Jeep roared up the street, honking. Jenny turned to see a big Boxer dog with his head hanging out of the window, barking. There was a large bird cage rocking on the back seat, holding a big, squawking, green and yellow parrot.

"Jenny, my love," Aunt Gertie called. She rolled into the driveway, opened the door, and hopped out. "Come meet Butch and Polly." She opened the hatch at the back of the Jeep.

"Hello! Hello!" the parrot squawked. "Bad dog! Bad dog!"

Jenny laughed. "What else can she say?"

"She says several things," Aunt Gertie answered. "She'll even repeat some of the things you say."

"Cool!"

"Bad dog! Bad dog! Squawk! Aark! @#%*! @#%*!"

"Did she say what I thought she said?" Jenny asked with her eyes wide.

"You heard it," Aunt Gertie said, laughing. "She picked up some bad language from her former owner. I've tried to break her from swearing, but she still does it when you least expect it."

At that moment Butch decided he wanted out of the Jeep. He jumped from the front seat to the back cargo space and to the ground at Jenny's feet in a matter of seconds. Jenny automatically put her hands behind her back and took a step backward. "Will he bite, Aunt Gertie?" Her eyes were wide.

"No, darling," she said, scratching Butch's ears. "He might lick you to death, though. Come and help me get these things into the house."

"Okay." Jenny picked up Polly's cage in one hand and a bag of dog food in the other.

Gertie carried two boxes and a small suitcase. She walked quickly, with Butch following closely at her heels.

"Argo, come see who's here!" Jenny called through the screen door. She set down the dog food so she could open the door.

"Hi, Gertie," Argo said coming to the door. "It's good to see you again. Your room is ready, right next to Jenny's. Oh, my! What's that?" she asked, looking at Butch.

"Meet Butch," Aunt Gertie said. Butch sat on the porch wiggling the stump of his tail.

"Is he a house dog or an outside dog?"

"House dog," Aunt Gertie answered.

"Oh, my!" Argo put her hand on her chest.

"Don't worry. You won't even know he's here," Aunt Gertie promised. "He's really very good."

"Bad dog! Bad dog! @#%*! @#%*!" Polly squawked.

"Oh, my!" Argo repeated. "Did she just say what I think she said?"

"I'm afraid so," Aunt Gertie said.

"Oh, my!" Argo said. "I hope the preacher doesn't come to call."

"If he does, I'll put her in my room," Aunt Gertie said.

"Oh, well," Argo said as she stepped out on the porch, "let's get the rest of your things and get you settled."

"Aunt Gertie!" Marylou called when Jenny and her aunt walked back out the front door. "When did you get here?" she asked, slinging her book bag to the porch floor.

"Just now, darling," Aunt Gertie answered. She grabbed Marylou and hugged her. "I'm so glad to see you! Look how tall you are." Aunt Gertie held her out at arm's length. "You've become a beautiful young lady."

"Beautiful! You think Marylou's beautiful?" Jenny couldn't believe what she had just heard. Sisters can't be beautiful. They're just sisters.

"Of course she is. She looks just like your mother," Aunt Gertie answered. "Come help us carry my things in from the car, then we can talk."

Argo carried a suitcase in each hand. Marylou carried two bags of fruits, vegetables, and whole wheat bread. Aunt Gertie put a box into Jenny's hands and said, "Be careful, it's my juicer." Marylou made a face, which made Jenny smile. "I'm glad you're so happy I brought it, dear. Maybe I can find one in town for Argo to use after I leave," she said as she turned around to get the parrot food and a box of shoes. "Well, I guess that's it," she said slamming down the back gate of the Jeep, missing Jenny's gagging look. She walked into the house and back to the kitchen.

"Oh, good. You have a place on the countertop for my juicer," Aunt Gertie said, as Jenny set it down in the space usually occupied by the microwave oven. "I'll clean these carrots and juice them with pineapple for supper."

"@#%*! @#%*! Squawk! Bad dog! Bad dog!" Polly squawked.

"What was that?" Marylou asked, turning around.

"That's Polly. She swears," Jenny announced.

"A swearing parrot! No way!" Marylou exclaimed with a grin on her face.

"I haven't figured out how to stop her, yet," Aunt Gertie told her. "I've only had her three months."

"Let's get your clothes up to your room and get you settled," Argo offered, changing the subject and picking up a suitcase.

Jenny, Marylou, and Aunt Gertie followed, each carrying an armload. Once in the room, Aunt Gertie looked around and exclaimed, "This is lovely, Argo! Did you do the decorating?"

"Yes, but I had lots of help," she said, winking at Jenny.

Aunt Gertie sat on the bed and exclaimed, "This is much too soft for my back. Would you mind if we slipped the mattress down on the floor and put the sheet on the box springs?"

"Why, Aunt Gertie?" Jenny and Marylou chorused.

"I can't sleep on soft mattresses. The box springs will work just fine." Argo, Jenny, and Marylou helped Aunt Gertie put the mattress on the floor. Butch took one look, stepped on the mattress, turned around three times, and then settled himself on the new bedspread.

"Oh, my!" Argo exclaimed. She put her hand on her chest.

"Butch, get off that lovely bedspread," Aunt Gertie cried. "Just because it's on the floor doesn't make it yours," she said, tugging on the dog's collar and pulling him off. "If you have an old sheet and blanket, we can protect the mattress from Butch," she told Argo.

Argo walked down the hall to the linen closet and came back with a plastic mattress cover and an old blanket. Together, Aunt Gertie and Marylou took off the bedding from the mattress and put it on the box springs. Then, Argo and Jenny slid the plastic cover on the mattress and laid the blanket on it. Butch settled back onto his 'new bed' and looked like he was smiling.

"I'm going downstairs to start dinner," Argo said, walking out the door shaking her head and muttering something about dogs and swearing parrots.

"What's for dinner, Argo?" Jenny asked, following her into the kitchen.

"Macaroni and cheese, peas, fruit salad, and, of course, Gertie's juice."

"Yuck, juice!" Jenny made a face and held her throat, very dramatically. "May we have chocolate pie, too?"

"Not until your Aunt Gertie leaves," she answered quietly.

* * * * * * * *

Dinner was lively, with Aunt Gertie doing much of the talking. "Do you have any boyfriends, Marylou?" she asked.

"No," Marylou answered.

"That's good. You'll have plenty of time for that later."

"Who would want *her* for a girlfriend, anyway?" Jenny asked, making a face.

"Jenny!" Argo said sharply.

Aunt Gertie turned toward her other niece and asked, "Jenny, what do you like to do?"

"I like to do lots of stuff. Calvin and I usually do most everything together."

"Calvin. Who's Calvin?"

"He lives next door," Jenny explained. "He's my best friend. He'll probably come over after dinner. Can he meet Butch and Polly?"

"Of course." Aunt Gertie dramatically put her hand to the front of her waist and bowed her head. "They'd be honored."

Jenny laughed, but Marylou just smiled.

After dinner, Mr. Jenkins was going out the door to go to the hardware store when Calvin ran up the porch steps. "Is Jenny home?" he asked.

"She's inside with her Aunt Gertie. I'll call her." He turned around. "Jenny! Calvin's here!"

When Jenny jumped up and ran to the door, Calvin asked, "Can you come out? I brought my soccer ball."

"I can't come out. My Aunt Gertie came this afternoon, and I have to stay in here. But, you can come in." She opened the screen door.

"Okay," Calvin answered, as he stepped into the house. He put his soccer ball on the floor under the coat rack.

"Bad dog! Bad dog! Squawk! @#%*! @#%*!" Polly called from the dining room.

"Is that Aunt Gertie?" he asked. His eyes were wide open in reaction to the swear words.

"No," Jenny laughed. "That's her parrot. She swears."

"Cool!" Calvin laughed. "A swearing parrot."

"Grr!" Butch growled at Calvin when he entered the living room.

"Oh, hush, Butch," Jenny scolded. "This is Calvin. He's a friend."

Calvin scratched the dog's ears. "Hi, Butch. I have a pretty girl dog at home. You'll like her." He turned to Jenny and asked, "Is he your Aunt Gertie's, too?"

"Yes." Then she yelled, "Aunt Gertie, Calvin's here!"

Aunt Gertie came in from the kitchen where she was helping Argo wash the dishes. She put out her hand to shake Calvin's. He seemed impressed that anyone would want to shake his hand.

"Calvin, I've heard lots of nice things about you. I'm glad you're Jenny's friend."

"Yeah. Me, too," Calvin answered. "She's fun to be with."

"I see you've met Butch and Polly."

"Yeah. Polly's cool."

"Eeek! Help!" Argo screamed from the living room. "What's that?"

Jenny ran toward Argo. "What's wrong?" she called out.

"Look!" Argo pointed toward the middle of the braided rug.

Calvin ran over to look. "It's just a tree frog."

"A frog! Get it out of here! Now!" Argo gripped the sides of a chair that was close by.

"What's the matter?" Marylou called as she ran down the stairs to see what was causing all the commotion.

"There's a frog in there!" Argo yelled at the top of her lungs. Her knuckles were white from squeezing the arms of the chair.

"A frog?" Marylou said. "All this yelling over a frog?"

"Help!" Argo yelled louder, stepping up on the little foot stool and waving her large arms.

"Why are you so scared? It's no bigger than a quarter," Aunt Gertie told her.

"But it's a frog!" Argo trembled. "I can't stand frogs! They terrify me."

The frog jumped over to the fireplace. Argo saw her chance and jumped off the stool. She ran out of the living room and into the kitchen where she grabbed a broom, then came running back. Jenny and Marylou had never seen her run that fast, ever. Swinging, she hit at the frog, which jumped frantically away just before the broom hit. It hopped under the open-back bookshelf. Sweeping the books off the shelf with the broom, Argo tried to hit it, but the frog jumped onto the rocking chair. Argo swung hard, hitting the rocking chair, but missing the frog. The chair sailed backwards, hit the window and broke it. Glass flew out onto the bushes in front of the house.

"Cool!" Calvin exclaimed.

"This is the funniest thing I have ever seen," Aunt Gertie howled, sinking to the floor on her knees.

"Argo, calm down." Marylou patted her on the back. "It's only a frog."

"I know! I know!" she cried, turning white. "I can't stand frogs! Ever since I was a little girl I've been scared of them. I even have nightmares about them."

By this time, Jenny and Calvin were holding their sides with their arms around their waists. Tears streamed down their cheeks from laughing so hard. They couldn't help themselves, as they watched Argo wildly chase a harmless little frog with a big broom. She ran all over the living room, swinging, hitting, missing, and swinging again. Butch joined in on the fun and chased around with Argo, barking the whole time. She hit the sofa, the chair, the end table, and the floor. She hit the lamp. It fell over, but Aunt Gertie raced over and caught it. The whole time, Argo was screaming at the top of her lungs.

Then, Argo ran out of the living room. She raced through the dining room, through the kitchen, and into the garage. She returned armed with a shovel that Mr. Jenkins kept hanging on the wall in the garage.

Aunt Gertie, still laughing, asked, "What *are* you going to do now?"

"I'm going to get that frog if it's the last thing I do! Where is it?"

"There it is!" Calvin yelled, pointing to the wall. The frog's sticky little feet were holding on to the wall, just below a picture of Jenny and Marylou's mother.

Argo drew back, the shovel over her shoulder like a baseball bat, and sized up the frog's position. She took a deep breath, swung, and hit the frog squarely on the back, squishing it against the wall and putting a shovel-sized hole in the wallboard.

"Cool!" Calvin exclaimed.

"Bad dog! Bad dog!" Polly squawked

"Oh, no!" Argo gasped, coming to her senses and looking at the hole. She put her hand on her chest. "What have I done?" Then, for the first time, she heard the dog barking and everyone laughing.

"It looks like you've punched a big hole in the wall, Argo," Aunt Gertie said, laughing with tears streaming down her cheeks. "I have never seen anything so funny."

"I guess I did overreact a little," Argo said.

"A little!" Aunt Gertie howled. She erupted in another fit of laughter.

"Frogs terrify me," Argo explained again.

"I can see that," Aunt Gertie continued laughing, wiping the tears from her eyes. "But why?"

"My grandmother's house was in a very low area. Frogs lived in the pond, under her porch, in her garden, everywhere. When I was very small, my mother would take me there, and frogs would jump all over me, on my legs, my arms, my clothes, and even get into my pockets to hop out and scare me when I would least expect it. When I crawled on her grass, they hopped up in my face, eyeball to eyeball. They seemed so slimy. I guess I never got over it. To this day, even a picture of a frog gives me chill bumps all over."

Mr. Jenkins came into the house. "What happened in here? It looks like a tornado roared through."

"A frog was in the living room," Jenny explained.

"Oh, no!" he said, turning toward Argo. "I know how terrified you are of frogs." He put his arm around her shoulders.

"I'm sorry," Argo said quietly. She looked down at the floor.

"It's all right," Mr. Jenkins said. He patted her back. "You can't help what you do when you're scared."

"I wish I had recorded it," Aunt Gertie said. "It was the funniest thing I've ever seen in my life."

Her make-up was smeared where tears had streamed down her face.

"I guess I'd better cover the widow. It's supposed to rain tonight," Mr. Jenkins said calmly, as he picked up the shovel to take it back to the garage. "I'll call Mr. Alexander, the town handyman, to come and repair the damage."

"Calvin," Marylou called from the kitchen, "your mom just phoned. She wants you to come home."

"Okay," he called back. "See you tomorrow, Jenny."

"Bye, Calvin," Aunt Gertie called. "It's been nice meeting you."

"Yeah, me too." Calvin picked up his soccer ball and opened the screen door.

"Bye, I'll see you tomorrow." Jenny called after him.

"Well, young ladies, it's almost bedtime. You need to take a shower," Argo told Jenny and Marylou. "Even if Aunt Gertie is here, you still have to go to school tomorrow."

"Will you drive us to school, Aunt Gertie?" Jenny asked.

"I'd love to. Maybe we can plan a fun weekend."

"Fun weekend?" Jenny asked.

"Maybe the three of us could go camping."

"Camping? We've never been camping before," Marylou told her.

"What? Your dad has never taken you camping? Your mom used to camp with him all the time. They even went camping on their honeymoon."

"On their honeymoon?" Marylou asked loudly? "Nobody goes camping on their honeymoon."

"They did. Isn't it incredible?"

"Maybe he doesn't want to go camping without Mom," Marylou said quietly.

"Maybe," Aunt Gertie said, "but it's high time you went. What kind of equipment do you have?"

"Equipment?" Jenny asked.

"Yes. Camping equipment."

"We don't have any," Jenny told her.

"Never mind. After I drop you off at school, I'll go get what we need. I'll talk to your dad tonight about it. I'm sure he won't object. Now scoot."

"Can Calvin come?" Jenny asked.

"Sure. Why not? Call him and ask him if he has a tent. Then let me talk to his mom."

"He doesn't have one," Jenny said. "He said one time he'd like to camp in his backyard, if he had a tent."

"Oh, well. Call him and ask him to come, anyway. We can leave after school. I'll get everything ready while you're gone."

"Okay," Jenny said, picking up the phone.

"What's up?" Mr. Jenkins asked, coming back into the room.

"Aunt Gertie wants to take us camping this weekend," Jenny said happily. "Please say yes, Daddy."

Mr. Jenkins rolled his eyes and thought, *'She must really want to go if she called me Daddy,'* I guess it's all right if you don't go too far. It's a shame I've never taken you, but I haven't felt much like camping since your mother died." He looked at Aunt Gertie and said, "We do have a big tent, some lanterns, and a camp stove. I packed all the camping gear away after your sister died. I guess the children don't know we have it."

After talking to Calvin, Jenny told Aunt Gertie, "He can go, but his mom wants to talk to you."

"Good," Aunt Gertie said taking the phone.

"Tomorrow is going to be wonderful," Jenny told Aunt Gertie. She turned and ran upstairs to take her shower.

Chapter Nine
The Campout

"I can't wait," Jenny told Calvin on the way home from school. "I'm so excited. Just think, I'm going camping for the first time in my life." She raised her shoulders, smiled, and shook her head,

"I've never been camping before, either," Calvin admitted, "except for one time in my Cousin David's backyard. He was so scared that we had to go in before midnight."

"Why was he scared?" Jenny asked.

"Some owls were hooting," Calvin said. "He thought they were ghosts."

"Owls don't sound like ghosts."

"To a little kid, they might," Calvin insisted.

"I just hope Marylou doesn't get scared. She's such a whuss! Look, there's Aunt Gertie packing the Jeep. I wonder what she bought today," Jenny said, breaking into a run.

"Hi, kids." Aunt Gertie turned toward them and smiled. "Are you ready to go?"

"Sure are," Jenny replied. "Where are we going to camp?"

"I checked into the places available for family camping and decided that I liked Stone Mountain Park the best. Is that all right with you?"

"Oh, good. I like that place. There's tons of things to do there."

"I like the laser show. Are we going to see that?" Calvin wanted to know.

"I haven't any definite plans once we get there. I guess if you kids want to see it, we could go tomorrow night," Aunt Gertie replied, smiling.

"I saw the campground last summer," Calvin said, "when we rode on the big riverboat ride around the lake. There's a beach next to the campground with an awesome slide that goes into the water, and there's paddleboats, and…"

"Can we do all that, Aunt Gertie?" Jenny asked.

"I don't see why not. We'll have two days and two nights out there."

"Did Argo pack my clothes?"

"Yes. She was taking your jeans out of the dryer when I came out. She said that was the last thing she had to put into your bag."

"I'll go home and get my things," Calvin said. He broke into a run as soon as he turned around.

"No hurry!" Aunt Gertie called after him. "We have to wait for Marylou to get home."

"Here's the cooler with some of the things you bought, Gertie," Argo said, coming out the front door and down the porch steps carrying a blue and white Igloo cooler. "The paper plates, plastic silverware, the bread and the cereals are in the box on the kitchen table."

"Thanks, Argo," Aunt Gertie said with a smile, taking the cooler. She put it in the back of the Jeep with the other gear. "Could I borrow your aluminum foil? We can bake potatoes and cook soup on the coals of the campfire with it."

"Make soup in aluminum foil on the campfire coals?" Jenny asked. "How?"

"You'll see," Aunt Gertie hinted, winking. "Oh, look. Here comes Marylou."

Marylou, after stepping off the school bus, walked over to the Jeep. "Mrs. Anderson is giving us a test on the parts of speech on Monday. Will I have time to study this weekend?"

"Of course. We'll make a game out of it tomorrow. Put your book in the Jeep now, so we don't forget it."

"Okay. I'll go get my clothes and be right back," Marylou said, throwing her English book on the back seat before heading for the house.

"Wait for me!" Jenny called, running after Marylou.

Calvin slammed his front door and ran next door to Jenny's house. "Here's my stuff," he said to Aunt Gertie. He had a green duffle bag in one hand and a sleeping bag in the other. "Mom's coming over with a box of food and a cooler of juice and milk. She said you knew about it."

"We made a grocery list together this morning. She wanted to help out with the food."

"Where's Jenny?" Calvin wondered, looking around.

"She's getting her things. Could you get the box on the kitchen table and put it in the Jeep?"

"Okay." He took off running to the Jenkins' house.

Mrs. Kelly walked up with a box and a cooler. "This sure is nice of you, Gertie."

"I'm looking forward to it. These are great kids, and I'm sure we're going to have a good time."

"Thanks. This will give me a chance to write an article on compost for the *Gardner's Magazine*. My deadline is next Wednesday," she said, putting the cooler and the box in the back of the Jeep.

"Here's Butch's food," Argo said. "I put it in a large Ziploc bag, so you wouldn't have to take the whole bag. It looks a bit crowded in there."

"Thanks. Are you sure you don't mind taking care of Polly? I cleaned her cage and left enough food to last through the weekend, I think."

"It's fine. I'll check on her food and water. I just hope the preacher doesn't come to call."

"We're ready," Jenny called out, running down the steps with her gym bag in one hand and her pillow in the other. Butch ran beside her with his tongue flapping as he ran. "Marylou will be out as soon as she says good-bye to Lisa."

"She's on the phone with Lisa?" Argo asked. "She just left her on the bus!"

"Not anymore," Jenny said. "Here she comes." She pointed toward the house.

"You kids will have to sit in the back seat. Butch likes to ride in the front," Aunt Gertie said, as she opened the front door. Butch leaped in and sat down looking pleased.

"That's cool," Calvin chuckled, climbing into the back, followed by the girls.

"We're off! Good-bye everyone," Aunt Gertie called, waving to Argo and Mrs. Kelly, as she backed out of the driveway.

"What's for supper?" Calvin asked. "Hamburgers or hot dogs?"

"Neither," Aunt Gertie replied.

"I thought that's what you ate when you camped."

"Not me. Just wait. You'll like it. If you're hungry now, there's a bag of apples behind you in the cargo space."

"Thanks," Calvin said. He reached behind him and grabbed an apple.

When they arrived at the park's gate, Aunt Gertie asked directions to the campground. As she was driving around the granite mountain, Aunt Gertie explained, "The first thing we need to do is put up the tent and put our things inside. It's a two room tent, so we should have plenty of space. I'll sleep in the room with Jenny and Marylou, and, Calvin, you can sleep in the room with Butch and our clothes. We'll leave the food in the Jeep until we need it. That way the animals won't get into it."

"Is the tent hard to put up?" Jenny asked.

"Not really, but, it will take all of us working together."

"That's cool," Calvin answered.

"Here's a good spot," Aunt Gertie said, stopping the Jeep and stepping out. "There's a water spigot nearby, the bathrooms are close, and the ground is fairly flat."

Calvin jumped out next with Jenny tumbling after him.

Aunt Gertie opened the back and pulled out a large blue tarpaulin and a new red–and-grey tent. "What's the tarp for?" Marylou asked.

"It's for ground cover, so we won't be sleeping on the damp ground."

"Oh. How do you know so much about camping?"

"Your mom and I used to camp with your grandparents every summer when we were kids. We sometimes even camped in the fall and winter."

"You camped in the winter?" Jenny gasped.

"That's when it's the most fun. There aren't any bugs, and you can sit around a big campfire, drinking hot cocoa, and toasting your toes."

"What about sleeping? Weren't you cold?" Marylou asked.

"Not really. We put hot water bottles in the bottom of our sleeping bags and kept warm all night."

"Cool," Calvin said.

"Let's spread out this tarp and put up the tent. Then we can start dinner," Aunt Gertie said as she carried the tarp over to the flat area. "Jenny and Calvin, will you please pick up those sticks and toss them aside?"

As fast as the children picked up the sticks and tossed them away from the tent area, Butch would pick them up and bring them back, wiggling his tail nonstop. "No, Butch! We're not playing fetch," Jenny protested. She laid down her sticks instead of tossing them. That seemed to work.

"Here's the tent," Marylou announced, walking up to Aunt Gertie with the tent across her arms. Aunt Gertie took it and pulled it out of the tent bag. After Calvin spread out the tarp, they all worked on the tent. Only two tries later, the tent was up. The sleeping bags, pillows, and clothes were put in their places, and Butch's blanket was put beside Calvin's things.

"I'm hungry!" Jenny complained.

"Let's start a fire," Aunt Gertie suggested. She laid fire starter and wood in the fire ring, and then lit it. "While we're getting the food ready, the fire will burn down into coals, then we can cook our soup."

"We didn't bring a big pot," Calvin pointed out. "How are we going to cook our soup?"

"Watch," Aunt Gertie replied. She folded the edges of aluminum foil, three layers thick, over three times on the bottom and three times on the sides, leaving the top open. She made four bowls, flattening out the bottom.

"Cool," Calvin said.

"Here, Marylou. Wrap these potatoes in foil and tuck them down in the bottom of the fire in the coals. They'll bake while we cook our soup," Aunt Gertie said, as she took out carrots, tomatoes, onions, and celery to cut up. She dropped them evenly into the four 'bowls' and added water, seasoning, noodles, and peas.

Soon the soup simmered, and the potatoes baked. The campers set their dishes on a cloth on the ground. Aunt Gertie filled Butch's bowl with dog food.

Later, Calvin dug the potatoes out of the fire with a big stick, and Aunt Gertie took the 'bowls' of soup off the fire and set them on paper plates.

"This is so-o-o good," Marylou said tasting the soup.

Jenny put some cheese on her baked potato and took a bite. "This is the best baked potato I've ever eaten."

"Me, too," Calvin added.

"Oh, I almost forgot. There's some fruit salad in the cooler," Aunt Gertie said, jumping up and walking over to her Jeep. "I made it this afternoon before you came home from school."

After everything was eaten, the 'dishes' thrown away, the fire put out, and the cloth folded up, Aunt Gertie sat on the edge of the small lake to watch the ducks. "Kids, come over here and watch this," she said pointing to the water.

"Watch what?" Jenny asked.

"Watch how the ducks land in the water. See that one coming down now?"

"Ruff. Ruff," Butch barked, his eyes fixed on the duck.

"Hush, Butch," Aunt Gertie scolded. "Watch the wings and the feet." She pointed to the stretched out wings that were as straight up and down as curtains on a window, and the toes on the feet that were pointing straight up.

"Cool," Calvin observed. "The wings look like flaps on an airplane when it's coming in for a landing."

"Their toes are straight up and their heels are pushing into the water like brakes!" Jenny cried.

"I've never noticed before how ducks land in the water," Marylou said, sitting down beside Aunt Gertie. "This is better than those wildlife shows on television."

After the duck show, Aunt Gertie suggested, "Let's go over to the beach area and check out what we can do tomorrow. It's still warm enough to go swimming. Fall doesn't officially start until next week."

Arriving at the beach, Calvin's eyes popped open. He yelled, "Look at that cool slide!" He pointed to a twenty foot tall, twisting and turning slide, which had a covered tube on the top two-thirds.

"I wish we could go on it now," Jenny sighed.

"The air is cooling off. We're better off waiting until tomorrow afternoon," Aunt Gertie advised.

"Let's walk back to the campsite," Marylou suggested.

By the time they got back, it was almost dark. "Let's light a fire and tell ghost stories," Jenny said.

"I know a good one about the ghosts of aliens who crashed into a forest in Canada," Aunt Gertie offered.

"Cool," Calvin piped once more.

After several ghost stories, one from each of the campers, except Butch, and eating apples cooked in molasses over the campfire, everyone was tired and ready for bed. The whispering of the night air, the lapping of the lake water against the shore, and the gentle hooting of the owls made a pleasant background for a good night's sleep.

The next morning, after eating cheese toast, toasted on a grate over the fire, cereal, and orange juice, Aunt Gertie drove to the paddleboats on the other side of the lake. Aunt Gertie rented two paddleboats and everyone put on life jackets. "Let's race," Jenny suggested. "Calvin and I can beat you two."

"You think so? You haven't seen 'Legs Gertie' in action," Aunt Gertie shot back. She tried Butch's leash to a stake in the grass and commanded, "Sit, Butch."

Jenny and Calvin climbed into their paddleboat. "Here are some sugar cubes I brought from home," Jenny whispered. "Eat some. They'll give you quick energy. We'll be sure to win."

"Cool," Calvin said using his favorite descriptive word, taking a handful.

Once everyone was in the lake, the two paddleboats lined up. "On your mark, get set, GO!" yelled Aunt Gertie. They took off, both boats were even for the first few yards. Gradually Jenny and Calvin gained the lead.

"Paddle faster!" Marylou shouted to Aunt Gertie.

"I can't," Aunt Gertie answered, huffing and puffing.

"Yea!" Jenny yelled. "We won by two boat lengths."

Tired of the boat race, the campers decided to take the tram, a bucket on a cable, up the steep side of the mountain, over the famous carving of Confederate soldiers on horseback. Butch hung his head out the open back window and barked. When the tram stopped at the top of the mountain, they got off and walked around. They saw the lake, the campground, and the Atlanta skyline.

"Look at those boys!" Jenny shrieked suddenly, pointing to two teenagers climbing over the chain-link fence that kept people from falling over the steep side of the mountain.

"What do they think they're doing? They'll be killed! Quick, Marylou, run and tell the guard by the gift shop!" Aunt Gertie yelled, pointing to where the tram had stopped. "I'll try to keep an eye on them."

"What are you going to do, Aunt Gertie?" Jenny stammered, running after her.

"I don't know. I do know that it's eight hundred feet down, and that *I'm* not going to take any chances."

As Jenny, Calvin and Aunt Gertie ran toward the fence, they heard, "Help! Help! Someone help!"

"That must be the boys," Aunt Gertie said, stopping at the fence. "Oh, my gosh! Look at those dark clouds. It's going to storm."

"If it rains hard enough, could the boys be washed over the edge?" Jenny asked.

"Sure could," Aunt Gertie answered, "especially if they're down in one of the cracks in the side. The water goes through them like a river when it rains."

"Look! A helicopter!" Calvin yelled, pointing up to a helicopter with Georgia State Patrol written on the side.

"That was quick. It must have been sitting here at the park," Aunt Gertie replied. "Listen."

"Attention! Boys, stay where you are! Don't move! We'll try to get you down," a loudspeaker from the helicopter announced.

"They must see the boys," Calvin said as he peered through the holes in the chain link fence, trying to get a better view.

Just then, the helicopter flew up and over the fence, landing behind Jenny, Calvin, and Aunt

Gertie. Three men in State Patrol uniforms jumped out, ducked, and ran over to where they stood.

"Ruff! Ruff!, Butch barked.

"Hush," Aunt Gertie scolded.

"You the folks that reported this?" one of the patrolmen asked.

"Yes," replied Aunt Gertie.

"Good work. We need to work fast. If it rains hard, those boys could be killed. They're halfway down one of those cracks and can't get up."

Just then, thunder clapped loudly. "Oh, no!" Jenny yelled.

"Please step back, folks. Go back to the building and watch from there," the patrolman said as he quickly cut the fence with a wire cutter. The other two patrolmen were running toward them, both wearing a harness around their waist and legs, which was attached to a rope that was unwinding from somewhere in the helicopter. Once they were through the hole in the fence, they turned around and walked backward right off the top of the mountain, the ropes holding them up.

"I hope they get to the boys in time," Aunt Gertie prayed, as she walked back to the building with Jenny and Calvin, saying a little prayer for their safety.

By this time, a crowd had gathered to watch the activities. The guard was walking back and forth in front of the crowd, warning them to stay back. Marylou came over to sit beside Aunt Gertie. She began to cry.

"Don't cry, honey. They'll get the boys," Aunt Gertie told her.

"Look!" Calvin shouted, pointing to one of the ropes that was reeling in slowly. "Someone's coming back."

Two heads appeared over the edge of the mountain, one of a Georgia State patrolman and one of a teen-age boy. The crowd cheered. Butch barked and wiggled his tiny little tail.

"Look over there!" Jenny yelled. Another set of heads came into view.

The crowd cheered louder. "Hooray! They rescued them!"

Butch barked louder.

By this time, two more helicopters appeared from different television stations. They were filming the rescue.

"Whew!" Jenny said with her hand on her chest. "That scared me!"

"I'll bet the boys were more scared," Aunt Gertie replied. "I don't think they'll try that again."

Calvin pointed to the fence. "Look, the guard is wiring the fence together."

"I guess he doesn't want any more excitement today. Maybe he thinks he could be blamed for not stopping the boys," Aunt Gertie said.

"It wasn't his fault the boys climbed the fence," Jenny said.

"No, but he might blame himself, anyway."

Suddenly, a microphone was shoved in front of Aunt Gertie. "I'm from Station WXTV. "Are you the ones who reported this?"

"Yes," Aunt Gertie replied.

"How did they get down there?"

"Jenny saw them first, ask her." Aunt Gertie said, pointing to her niece.

Jenny told the reporter everything that happened, how quickly the State Patrol got there, everything. She wasn't nervous until the interview ended.

After the newsmen left, Aunt Gertie suggested that they leave the mountain top. "Let's take the tram back down and ride the train. I'd like to get off the mountain before it storms."

On the way down, Jenny looked for the crack in which the boys were stuck. "It's probably that one over there," she said, pointing to a large crack that started out very large, but came to a point at the bottom. It was just big enough for someone to crawl in.

"Once they were in it, it would be hard to climb straight up to get out," Aunt Gertie said quietly.

Once on the ground, they hurried over to the train, which was just about to depart. Aunt Gertie bought four tickets and promised the ticket agent that Butch would be good. As soon as they sat down, the storm broke, sending large drops that bounced off the train windows. The rain came down hard and fast, lasting the whole trip. But, as soon as they arrived back at their station, the clouds parted, and the sun began to streak through. Jenny and Calvin jumped off the train and put pennies on the track for the train wheels to flatten when they started to roll again.

The train whistle shrilled. The wheels moved forward slowly. Gradually, they picked up speed. The five cars and the engine were pulling away from the station. Jenny and Calvin ran to check on their pennies.

"Cool!" Calvin exclaimed, as he picked up the pennies flattened out in oval shapes.

"I'm hungry," Marylou complained.

"Me, too," Jenny echoed. "Let's go back to camp and eat lunch."

"Good idea," Aunt Gertie said. "Last one back to the Jeep is a rotten egg," she yelled, breaking into a run.

After they ate a lunch of peanut butter sandwiches, apples, and milk, they all changed into their bathing suits and spent the afternoon swimming and sliding.

"I sure am having fun!" Jenny exclaimed.

"Me, too," Marylou added, falling back on her beach towel, sighing. "I wish this could last forever."

"It's getting cool," Aunt Gertie said, getting up. "Let's go back to the campsite and eat supper."

After a meal of tomato sandwiches, mushroom soup, and fresh pineapple, everyone was feeling better. "Let's go see the laser show at the base of the mountain," Aunt Gertie suggested. "This is the last night it's going to be shown until next spring."

"I've heard about the laser show," Calvin said. "My cousin, Kenny, told me about the cool colors that streak through the air and make pictures on the side of the mountain."

"I went one time last year with Lisa and her family," Marylou said. "It's beautiful."

"It's starting to get dark," Aunt Gertie said. "Let's grab a blanket to sit on and go."

The laser show was beautiful, with light beams in different colors that cut across the night sky. They came to rest on the side of the granite mountain, forming pictures that changed so quickly that Jenny was afraid to blink for fear she might miss something. Even Butch seemed to like the show, or maybe it was the girl Boxer on the next blanket.

"Cool!" Calvin said over and over again.

Back at the campsite, everyone was so tired that they crawled right into their sleeping bags. Butch cuddled up to Calvin, laying his head on his legs.

"Night, everyone," Jenny said sleepily.

"Night," Marylou, Calvin, and Aunt Gertie chorused.

In the morning, after the church service on the top of the mountain, Aunt Gertie suggested, "Let's take a ride on the big riverboat around the lake before we go home."

"Can we ride on the top deck?" Jenny asked.

"Okay, if no one objects," Aunt Gertie answered. "I hope they let Butch on the boat."

"I'll pretend I'm blind and Butch is my lead dog," Calvin suggested.

"I'm sure he can get on," Aunt Gertie said. Butch got on, and he behaved himself.

Early in the afternoon, Aunt Gertie, Jenny, Calvin, Marylou, and Butch broke camp and packed everything up. "This has been fun," Jenny sighed. "Thanks, Aunt Gertie for taking us."

"You're welcome, darling. I've had a good time, too. It's been good to get to know you both better, and, of course, to get to know Calvin," she said, smiling.

"You're not as weird as I thought you were," Jenny said.

"Jenny!" Marylou said sharply.

"It's all right, Marylou. I know that the rest of the family thinks I'm a little strange, because I do what I want and not what they always want me to do. Your mother thought I should have settled down and married, like she did. That's not the life for me."

"We like you just the way you are, Aunt Gertie," Jenny said, hugging her.

"Oh, no! I forgot to study for my English test," Marylou wailed.

"We can study on the way," Aunt Gertie suggested. "It'll take us an hour to get there, so there will be plenty of time."

"Thanks, Aunt Gertie. You've made this weekend so much fun."

"Where's Butch?" Aunt Gertie asked. "He's not on his chain."

"I saw him run over by that camping trailer," Calvin said, pointing.

"Look!" Marylou yelled. "He's over by that girl Boxer we saw last night on the next blanket."

Aunt Gertie, Jenny, Marylou, and Calvin walked over to the next campsite. "Hello. Is my dog bothering you? I didn't know he was loose," Aunt Gertie said to a tall, blonde-haired man standing beside the girl Boxer.

"Not at all," he answered. "I love dogs. This is Taffy."

Aunt Gertie bent down, shook the Boxer's paw and smiled, "I'm glad to meet you, Taffy. Butch certainly has good taste."

Butch sat down beside his friend and looked like he was smiling.

"I'm Brad Perkins," the man introduced himself, extending his hand.

"Nice to meet you. I'm Gertie Anderson, owner of the runaway," she said smiling, shaking his hand and nodding toward Butch. "These are my nieces, Marylou and Jenny, and Jenny's friend, Calvin."

"Nice to meet you all," Brad Perkins said, shaking Calvin's hand. "Do you live around here?" he asked, looking at Aunt Gertie. "It's nice to meet another Boxer lover....," Brad continued, walking toward the lake with Aunt Gertie.

"He sure is handsome," Marylou commented. "Maybe Aunt Gertie will change her mind about men, if he likes her."

"You know what? We haven't had any desserts or meat this whole weekend," Jenny said. "I've had so much fun, I've hardly noticed."

"Me, too," Calvin said. "I'm glad she let me come."

"I am, too," Jenny sighed.

"Look, Aunt Gertie's coming back, and they're both smiling," Marylou pointed out. "She sure is pretty when she smiles like that."

"It looks like Brad thinks so, too," Jenny said.

"Let's go, kids." "Your dad," she said looking at Jenny and Marylou, "and your mom," she said, looking at Calvin, "are going to be worried. I told them that we'd be home by four o'clock."

"Are you going to see Brad again?" Marylou asked.

"I might. We exchanged phone numbers."

"Yes!" Marylou said, smiling and making a fist with her hand in the air and shoving her elbow down sharply.

The ride home was spent playing a game using different parts of speech. Everyone was an expert on the subject by the time they pulled into the driveway.

"It's been fun, but it's good to be home, too," Jenny said, opening the door.

Argo met them at the door. "I saw you all on the news. Jenny, you were wonderful! You didn't look nervous at all. Maybe you'll be a reporter when you grow up."

Jenny laughed. "I don't think so, Argo. I want to do something that involves music."

"Oh, well," Argo sighed quietly, so much for knowing someone famous."

The children and Aunt Gertie laughed.

Chapter Ten

Departure

"I wish you didn't have to leave, Aunt Gertie. It's been so much fun having you here," Jenny said at breakfast Tuesday morning.

"Bad dog! Bad dog!" Polly squawked.

"Oh, I didn't forget you, Polly," Jenny said turning around to face her cage. "I'll miss you, too."

"Did you hear that?" Marylou yelled excitedly.

"Hear what?" Jenny asked.

"Polly didn't swear!"

"I know why," Argo said.

"Why?" Jenny, Marylou, and Aunt Gertie chorused.

"Well, I did to her what I did to Snoopy when he clawed the furniture."

"Who's Snoopy?" Aunt Gertie asked.

"Snoopy's the cat we used to have," Jenny answered. "He died."

"Argo, did you kill Snoopy? What did you do to Polly?" Aunt Gertie asked worriedly.

"Relax, Gertie. I didn't kill Snoopy, and I didn't hurt Polly. Snoopy died of old age. The cure-all is water."

"Water?"

"Yes. Every time Polly swore this weekend, I'd squirt her with a water gun. I only squirted her when the bad words came out. By Sunday, she only said words that even the preacher would approve."

"Wow! Argo, that's fantastic! Thanks," Aunt Gertie said.

"Can't you stay any longer, Aunt Gertie?" Marylou asked.

"No, darling. I really can't. Tomorrow I start my new job."

"What kind of new job?" Jenny asked.

"I'm going to tag bears in the Smoky Mountain National Park."

"Tag bears?" What do you have to do?" Marylou asked.

"I'll be going into the park with other taggers, tranquilize the bears with no tags in their ears, and clip in a bright orange tag."

"Isn't that dangerous?" Argo asked.

"Not really, if you don't try to tag the babies with their mom standing over you."

"Why tag them?" Jenny asked.

"To keep track of how many there are and where they roam. There's a lot of record keeping. If one we tagged near Cherokee ends up in Knoxville, we'll know to which area to take him back. Or, if one is found to be too wild for the park and is dangerous around people, we'll know which bear to look for to remove it to a very remote area. There are a lot of reasons."

"It sounds exciting!" Jenny said. "How can you find a bear if you need him?"

"There's a little sound sensor in each of the tags. The bears can be tracked by its beeps from a helicopter. Well it's getting late. I need to get started, and you two need to go to school."

"Where are you going to put everything?" Argo asked. "Your Jeep was full when you came, and you bought all that camping equipment."

"Oh, I'm leaving all that. Maybe it'll help to get Jim camping again. He needs to take the girls."

"He can take them all he wants," Argo said with her hands on her hips, "as long as I don't have to go. Sleeping on the ground with worms, bugs, and frogs is not my idea of a good time. Girls, help your Aunt Gertie carry her things out to the Jeep." She picked up the bag of dog food and the box containing the juicer, then walked out the door.

"Okay," they both said. Jenny carried the parrot cage and Aunt Gertie's make-up bag. Marylou took the bag filled with Butch's bowls and doggie treats in one arm and a suitcase with the other hand.

As soon as everyone was out the door, Calvin came running across the yard. "What's up?" he asked.

"Aunt Gertie's leaving. She starts a new job tomorrow, tagging bears," Jenny answered.

"Cool! I never knew anyone who did that."

Butch ran over to Calvin. "Woof!" he barked, licking his hand.

"Bye, yourself," Calvin said. He reached down and hugged Butch. "I'll miss you."

"We'll be back to visit," Aunt Gertie told him, "if they let us come."

"Of course, Gertie. You're welcome anytime. You can come for Thanksgiving, if you can stand to see us eat turkey," Argo said.

"Thanksgiving's out. I'm going skiing in Colorado that weekend," she said, putting the last box into the back of the Jeep and closing the hatch. She opened the front door, and Butch jumped in, looking like he was smiling.

"Bad dog! Bad dog!" Polly squawked as she was put on the back seat. Jenny and Calvin laughed "I'm off," Aunt Gertie said, as she hugged the three children. "Say good-bye to Jim for me." She climbed into the Jeep, opened the window and blew a kiss. She backed out of the driveway, waving. Once on the street, she squealed her tires and took off, with Butch barking and Polly squawking.

"Cool!" Calvin said.

"You three need to run and get your book bags," Argo said. "You don't need to be late for school."

After school, Jenny ran to find Argo. "What's for supper, Argo? I hope its hamburgers."

Marylou got off her bus and ran to find Argo. "Could we please have chocolate cake for supper?"

"I guess we all could use a treat," Argo agreed. "Will you help?"

"Sure," Marylou answered. "What can I do?"

"I'll bake the cake, and you can get the grill ready."

"Can Calvin stay for supper?" Jenny asked.

"I don't see why not. We have plenty of hamburger meat. Ask his mother if she would like to join us, too."

"Okay, thanks. Come on, Calvin," Jenny said, darting across the yard.

"Wait up!" Calvin called following her.

By the time they got back, Marylou was lighting the charcoal. "I've done this, now you can clean the grill with the wire brush."

"Okay," Jenny answered.

Mr. Jenkins drove into the driveway. "Hi, kids. Where's Gertie? I don't see her Jeep," he said as he stepped out of the car.

"She left. She's starting a new job tomorrow," Jenny answered.

"That's right. Tagging bears," he said with a smile. "You never know what to expect from her. What are we grilling for supper?" he asked, looking at Jenny.

"Hamburgers," she said with a smile.

"Oh, you're home, Jim," Argo said, coming out on the back porch. "Would you please carry the microwave in from the garage and put it back in the kitchen?"

"Sure. I'll go change clothes, first."

"Jenny, you and Calvin can make the hamburger patties, but wash your hands first."

"Okay," Jenny answered. The two friends ran into the house.

"Mmm, the cake sure smells good," Calvin said, licking his lips.

"Argo makes the best cakes, ever," Jenny told him.

After supper, Calvin went to get his football and asked Jenny to play catch. Marylou was talking on the phone to Lisa. Mr. Jenkins, Argo, and Mrs. Kelly sat and talked on the back porch.

"It was nice having Gertie for a short time, but I sure missed having meat," Mr. Jenkins said.

"It was wonderful what she did for the kids last weekend," Mrs. Kelly said. "Calvin couldn't stop talking about it."

"She seems to have some strange ideas, but she just might be right about some of them," Argo admitted.

"I'm sure some of her ideas have credibility," Mr. Jenkins said, but I'm not ready to do what she does just yet."

After a few minutes of tossing the football back and forth, with Buffy chasing it each time they threw it, Jenny and Calvin sat down on the back porch steps. "It's the official last day of summer," Jenny said. Fall starts tomorrow."

"It's weird that it's September and it still feels like summer," Calvin answered.

"It's been a fun summer and a sad one, too," Jenny said sadly.

"Yeah, with your uncle dying just after school started," Calvin said.

"I miss Uncle Paul. I'm glad you were here. You kept me from being so sad. Let's always be best friends."

"I've never had a best friend before you moved next door. It's cool."

"I can tell you things and talk about stuff that I never could tell anyone else. Marylou laughs at me, my girlfriends only want to talk about themselves, and Argo and Dad really don't listen when I talk like you do."

"Yeah, I know what you mean," Calvin answered. "You like to do cool stuff. You're not like the other girls."

"Thanks," Jenny said with a smile. "You're the only one who understands me, who knows how I feel."

"We sure had a cool time with your Aunt Gertie. Was your mom like her?"

"I don't remember, but from the way Dad and Marylou talk about her, I don't think so."

"It must be weird not having a mom."

"Not really. Argo is just like a real mom. She does everything your mom does."

"She cooks cool food, too," Calvin said. "Maybe your dad will marry her. Then she'll be your mom."

Jenny laughed. "She'd have to lose some weight first."

"We can work on your dad and my mom," Calvin suggested. "Then you can be my sister."

"Well,...maybe, but I'm happy with things just the way they are, as long as we stay friends. Let's see if there's any ice cream in the freezer," Jenny said, getting up.

"Cool." Calvin grinned and followed her.

Epilogue

Jenny and Calvin did stay best friends for a long, long time. Even though they went their different ways, Jenny to a music academy and Calvin to an architecture college, they still kept in touch with each other. They got together on holidays and summer break and caught up on each other's lives.

When Calvin fell in love, not surprisingly, the girl resembled Jenny. She had the same sunny outlook on life and was willing to do anything new and exciting. Jenny was genuinely happy for them both.

Jenny eventually married another musician. They traveled all over America sharing their love for music and telling people about their experiences with people who were about to pass on, and, in rare cases have passed on, telling what they had learned from them about Heaven.

About The Author

Ann Westmoreland lives near a small town west of Atlanta, Georgia. She grew up in Northern Illinois, graduated from Rockford College with a master's degree in elementary education, and taught elementary school in Illinois, then moved to Georgia, and taught until she retired. She is married with four children, six grandchildren, and two great-grandsons.